Jessica's Trap

By
H. K. Hillman

EP

Eternal Press
A division of Damnation Books, LLC.
P.O. Box 3931
Santa Rosa, CA 95402-9998
www.eternalpress.biz

Jessica's Trap
by H. K. Hillman

Digital ISBN: 978-1-61572-369-0
Print ISBN: 978-1-61572-370-6

Cover art by: Dawné Dominique
Edited by: Heather Williams
Copyedited by: Michelle Ganter

Copyright 2011 H. K. Hillman

Printed in the United States of America
Worldwide Electronic & Digital Rights
1st North American and UK Print Rights

All rights reserved. No part of this book may be reproduced, scanned or distributed in any form, including digital and electronic or mechanical, including photocopying, recording, or by any information storage and retrieval system, without the prior written consent of the Publisher, except for brief quotes for use in reviews.

This book is a work of fiction. Characters, names, places and incidents either are the product of the author's imagination or are used fictitiously, and any resemblance to any actual persons, living or dead, events, or locales is entirely coincidental.

Chapter One

April 30th, 1647

Simon Bulcock moved along the dark forest pathways with a poacher's practiced ease. He slid between trees and bushes without dislodging so much as a dewdrop from their branches.

Although he carried a lantern, he preferred not to use it. Others might see the light, and capture would mean a spell in the pillory, maybe even prison. The owner of this land, Lord West, had changed during Simon's absence from the village. Once a kind and fair landowner, he had become moody and intolerant.

Simon paused to catch his breath. The civil war had changed many things. There was more violence in the world now than at any time in Simon's past, so the increased severity of Lord West's justice was only to be expected.

A cloud hid the moon. Trees merged with the night. Simon squinted into the gloom, cursing the toll the years had taken on his sight. With care, he continued on his way, determined to deliver his message. His lantern, hidden beneath his coat, pressed into his side. Simon considered lighting it but decided to press on without its help. The risk was too great tonight.

The four rabbits and one hare hanging from Simon's belt spoke of a good evening's catch. He had meat to spare tonight, and he knew someone who would appreciate a share of his bounty. He needed to speak to Jessica anyway, to tell her what he had just heard.

The effort of staring into the darkness made Simon's head ache. He stopped walking and sat on a fallen tree to rest. Poaching was a young man's game, and it was one Simon had played for a very long time. He pushed his long, thinning, gray hair back from his face and took a few slow breaths. Pure forest air filled his lungs. This was the reason Simon had never settled for a life in town. The stink of people living too close together repelled him, although he forced himself to bear it during his visits to the tavern. To Simon, time spent in the forest was never time wasted. Poaching brought little income, but Simon's needs were few.

His simple life had become more difficult with the passing

years. Simon could still outrun that overfed, self-important fool of a bailiff when he needed to, but the exercise hurt him these days.

Something rustled the grass beside him. Simon followed the unseen creature's progress. Too small for a rabbit, possibly a mouse or shrew. Not big enough for the pot, whatever it was. His thoughts turned to Jessica, the girl he was to visit. Simon still thought of Jessica as a girl but he knew he should refer to her as a woman, now she had grown.

She had never really joined the village, but that was more his fault than hers. With both her parents gone, Simon had worried that her family's past would be remembered, so he had advised her to keep to herself.

That had been a mistake, he now knew. Her isolation only made the villagers suspicious. Their suspicions were partly correct, but it was their interpretation of those suspicions that concerned Simon.

The fire was still fresh in Simon's memory—the flames that had burned Jessica's mother, years ago. Her screams still reverberated in his ears; the sight of her struggling against her bonds still seared his dreams.

It was Simon who had helped Jessica and her father flee, Simon who had brought them here, to the village of his birth. He was indebted to Jessica's mother, and he had sworn to take care of her family. He had failed Jessica's father. He must not fail Jessica.

The full moon emerged from the sparse clouds to illuminate Simon's world. He rose to his feet. It was unwise to remain in clear view, so close to the main path and in such bright light. Simon slipped deeper into the woods and took the long route to Jessica's house.

A twig snapped under his foot, the crack loud in the stillness. Simon held his breath. An owl hooted in the distance. A scurrying in the bushes beside him signaled the flight of some frightened animal. Simon wiped a thin film of sweat from his brow with the coarse sleeve of his long coat. He waited and listened as the night creatures resumed their business. Satisfied that the twig had drawn no unwelcome attention, he continued on his way.

It was late to call on Jessica. Simon guessed it must be close to midnight, and she might be already asleep. Nonetheless, he had to speak to her tonight. The warning he carried could not wait until morning. Simon hoped to persuade her to move closer to the village, to stay with him for a while.

It was contrary to all his advice over the years, but times

change. The villagers believed she was his niece, so the arrangement should not strike them as odd. In these times, a woman living alone was at great risk, from many dangers.

Light gleamed in the trees ahead. Simon moved with caution until he had a clear view of Jessica's cottage. A plain white sheet covered the window, diffusing the light from within. So, she was still awake.

Even by moonlight, the cottage looked terrible. Jessica's father, Simon's friend, had done his best but he was a farmer, not a builder. Even with Simon's help, and with the advice of the local carpenter, the building seemed to stay up more by good fortune than by design. The walls, a ramshackle arrangement of locally obtained rocks, tilted inwards. The roof at least was straight, thanks to the intervention of the village carpenter. However, inexperienced hands had thatched it, and a few holes now showed as dark patches among the straw.

There remained much to do to make the cottage habitable, but Jessica's father was gone now and Simon was too old to be carrying stones and climbing walls. Shaking his head, Simon left the safety of the trees and crossed the rutted track to the cottage.

Chapter Two

Jessica Chadwick dropped the small book and gaped at the apparition before her. Her black cat, Belson, brushed past her legs.

"Belson. Don't." Jessica clasped her hands as the cat ran to the specter and sat before it.

"What have you done?" The voice, thin and distant, was unmistakably that of Jessica's mother. "Your father should have destroyed my book, should have hidden your abilities from you. Jessica, you are meddling in dangerous games and you have no training, no guidance."

"Mother? Is it really you?" Jessica took a hesitant step forward.

"If it were not me, you would be dead now." The spirit's lips twisted into a scowl. "You have made no preparations. Where is your circle of protection? Where is your triangle, to contain and control the spirits you call?" The ghost of Jessica's mother shook her head.

"I have never called a spirit before. I didn't really believe it would work."

"So you have meddled with my Book of Shadows without knowing what you were doing?" The specter drifted forward, over Belson, until it hovered a few feet from Jessica. "You were lucky, the things that could have answered..."

"I'm not a fool, Mother. I've practiced the lesser magics for years, since Father was taken by the soldiers." Jessica fought the tremble in her lip as she spoke. This close, her mother was both terrifying and beautiful. The rough walls showed through the white robes covering the specter's body, their uneven stones rippling with the movement of her limbs. "I didn't just start with this spell."

"I see." The ghost nodded. "It seems blood will out, after all. You have chosen a bad time to come into your power, my dear. War and plague blight the land, and the people look for someone to blame. If they catch you, they will kill you."

"I know. I need your help."

"I am dead, Jessica. There is little I can do." The ghost looked down at the black cat purring beside her. "Belson will be of more help to you than I."

"Mother, please. Belson is only a cat. I need advice. I'm alone now. There's a Witchfinder in the land. I don't want to be hanged." Jessica tried to grasp at the ghost's clothing, but her mother backed away.

"Alone? What about Simon Bulcock?"

"He still looks after me, but he's old. His strength is fading."

Jessica's mother looked around at the single room of the cottage. She grimaced at the sheet covering the window, held in place by sticks pushed between the stones of the wall. She shook her head at the rickety table and two chairs, and sighed at the single low bed and battered cabinet in the corner. The cooking pots beside the fireplace were blackened and worn. The night sky showed through holes in the roof. A wooden pail stood beneath one of the larger holes. The floor, though dry at the moment, consisted of hard-packed soil. Depressions in its surface suggested the formation of puddles whenever it rained.

"You have a hard life, it seems, and only seventeen. I know your father's farm was forfeit when I was condemned. I watched your flight from our comfortable home. I could not intervene, and cannot now, but I can answer some of your questions." Her semi-transparent features formed a smile.

"Then tell me about the Witchfinder. How can I escape his attention?"

"You cannot." The specter wavered in anger, or perhaps despair. "The creature within him will find you, now that your power is alive within you. You must call on help."

"Help? From who?"

"I suggest you call the one who was most sympathetic to me in my life. His name is Foras. The calling will not be easy—"

"That's one of the demons in this book." Jessica ran to the table and opened a heavy, leather-bound manuscript.

"You have the Goetia? How?" Her mother drifted alongside.

"I—ah—borrowed it from the monks at Marchway."

"Jessica, you are surely my daughter." The ghost laughed. "I would have given much to own the whole book. As it was, I paid a great deal to obtain copies of a few pages, and those burned with me."

Jessica turned the pages slowly, avoiding her mother's gaze. She had not witnessed her mother's death, but she overheard her father and Simon discussing it. They mentioned a betrayal, and a name. Jessica looked up.

"Mother." Jessica paused, her mind hunting for the words to ask what she wanted to know. "Who is Demdike?"

"That name should be forgotten." Her mother's face became stern. "Or perhaps not. Demdike is the man who betrayed me to the Inquisitor. Beware that name, Jessica. With luck, you will never hear it again."

"Father said the same, though Simon thought him innocent. Can Foras kill this Demdike also?"

"Ask Foras only one favor at a time, and be sure you know the demon's price before you agree. Forget about Demdike. You have more pressing problems. The creature hunting witches, the one you call Witchfinder, is one of the Golab. It possesses men's bodies, and feeds on the terror of women. The life within you would be a feast for it. You cannot fight it alone. Foras can help, if he will."

"If he will? You mean he may not?"

"Calling demons is a risky thing, Jessica. They don't always do what you expect of them. That is why you need the circle, and the triangle. And Belson, of course."

"Belson?" Jessica stared at the cat. It had been with the family as long as she could remember, so it must be at least as old as her. She had never before thought to question how Belson stayed so fit and healthy. Jessica turned her gaze to her mother.

"My familiar. Yours, now. Trust him, he is known to Foras and can be of assistance to you." The ghost drifted backwards, fading.

"Mother, wait. Don't leave. There is so much I need to know."

"I have no choice. Your spell was poorly cast. Its hold weakens."

"Wait. What about this Golab? How do I kill it?" Jessica moved toward her mother's ghost, now barely visible.

A short laugh echoed, as though along a tunnel. "If I knew that, I would have killed it before it killed me. Call Foras, but take care." The specter dissipated into the air, leaving a scent Jessica remembered from her childhood. Her mother's scent.

Jessica sank to her knees. If she could not hold on to her mother's ghost, what chance did she have of controlling Foras, a President of Hell? Belson sat on the floor in front of her, his head tilted to one side.

"Belson, are you really a spirit familiar? Can you help me?"

Belson ran to the table, jumped onto it and pushed at the pages of the open book with his paw. Jessica retrieved her mother's small spell book from the floor and joined Belson at the table. Belson had turned a few pages, and now rested his paw on the book. Jessica read the text he indicated.

The thirty-first spirit is Foras.

She stared at the page, then at Belson. "All this time, I thought you no more than a cat." She placed her mother's book on the table and sat down to read Goetia. Moonlight shafted through the holes in the roof, illuminating small patches of the bare floor. Jessica noted the distance between a particular patch of light and a mark she had made in the floor, a long time ago.

"It's close to midnight, Belson, and tonight is Beltane eve. There will be no better time for magic for some months. We must hurry, if we are to prepare to call this demon."

The tap at the door was so soft, Jessica hardly registered it at first. Then, a low voice called her name. She looked up.

"Simon. Oh, not now." Jessica briefly considered pretending to be asleep but he would have seen the candlelight through the window. She closed Goetia, slid both books under her bed, and went to the door.

Chapter Three

"Jessica." Simon hissed the word through the cracks in the door. He knocked again, checking the path both ways as he did so. There was no telling when the bailiff, or a troop of Cromwell's soldiers would pass by.

With the civil war all but over, there should be nothing to fear, but Parliament had refused to pay its army. The soldiers were angry and unpredictable. The sound of the wooden bar sliding away, behind the door, brought a sigh of relief from Simon.

The door swung inwards to reveal an interior barely more illuminated than the moonlit night outside. A familiar perfume drifted on the air. Simon inhaled, searching his memory for a link. Simon stepped inside and helped Jessica bar the door. He stood back, admiring her for a moment.

Jessica stood as tall as Simon. Her slender body was covered with a simple white woolen gown, flame-red hair, like her mother's, cascaded over her shoulders. Simon thought of the time when she was small, and he was a younger man. If only he were a young man now.

Simon shook his head to clear it of such thoughts. His lot was to take care of Jessica, not take advantage.

"It's late, Simon." Jessica's voice held a trace of impatience.

"Yes. I'm sorry. I brought fresh-caught rabbits." Simon opened his coat and untied two rabbits from his belt. "I didn't want to carry them around in daylight."

"Thank you, Simon." Jessica took the rabbits and laid them on the table. "I'm afraid I can't offer you anything in return."

"There's no need." Simon took a deep breath. "I really came to warn you, there are soldiers close by. I heard tonight. Roundheads."

"I thought the war was over."

"Maybe. There's more trouble brewing. Over in Marchway, just a few miles from here, there's a camp. The soldiers are heading for London. They might pass this way." Simon grimaced. "They'll be drinking up all the monks' best ale."

"I'm sure the monks will brew more. It's Mayday tomorrow, remember. There'll be plenty of ale in the tavern." Jessica glanced at her bed. "I don't want to turn you away, but..."

"That's all right, Jessica. I understand." Simon shuffled his feet. "I was thinking, maybe it would be better if you stayed at my house tonight. Safer, you know? It's closer to the village. The soldiers will be drunk, and they're not in the best of moods anyway."

"I like it here. Don't worry about me." Jessica slid back the bar from the door.

"I know it's your father's house and all, but just for tonight? I'd sleep easier, knowing you were safe."

"I'm as safe here as I'd be in the village. Safer, maybe. You know many of those people treat me with suspicion."

Simon winced. He had seen Jessica cook without fire, heal wounds and fevers with herbs, even make some small things invisible. She had not developed her powers to the same extent as her mother, but Simon envied Jessica, as he had envied Jessica's mother, and others before her.

"They're happy to take your help when they're sick."

"Yes, but they're afraid of me. As long as I stay out of their way, they'll leave me alone. Goodnight, Simon." Jessica opened the door. The perfume wafted through the air again. Simon sniffed at the familiar scent. It troubled him, it nagged at memories he preferred to leave alone.

"Please, Jessica? You'd be safer with me. At least until the soldiers have gone."

"I'm sure you have no reason to worry, Simon." Jessica held the door open, allowing the night breeze to fill the house. The perfume faded among the smells of the forest.

"I'll come back early in the morning, then. Just to be sure." He stepped through the door as he spoke.

"If you like. Though I think you may be lured away by the promise of ale." Jessica winked and tapped his arm. "It's not like you to miss a minute of the festivities. Besides, I'll be there myself, selling my herbs. Good night, Simon." She closed the door.

Simon faced the worn wood, seeing faces in the knots on its surface. He took a step backwards and stopped. The perfume belonged to Jessica's mother. It had been years since he last smelled it, but he was certain. Thyme and rosemary were her favorite herbs. Their scent had filled her hair and her clothes.

Tomorrow was Mayday. Simon had forgotten. Which meant tonight was Beltane, an important night for a witch. How far, he wondered, had Jessica's knowledge grown? Did she call spirits now?

If Jessica had called up her mother's spirit, then she must have reached the point Nicholas, his teacher, had warned him about. The point where she needed guidance, before she harmed herself with untrained magic. Simon slipped back into the woods, where he could watch the cottage unseen. Envy gripped his heart, while fear churned his stomach.

Jessica's magic came naturally. It was hers from birth. Despite his long association with practitioners of these arts, Simon had developed no power of his own. Even under the tutelage of Nicholas, Simon could manage little more than to lure rabbits into his traps, and that was more due to the potions he had learned to create than to any power of his own mind. Simon pushed his envy aside. His priority must be Jessica.

His fear remained. It was clear from Jessica's manner that Elizabeth had not revealed what he had done. Simon's guilt was still hidden, but for how long? Now that Jessica had access to her mother, his secret was no longer his alone. It might be better to tell Jessica himself, but he could not. Such an act required courage, and Simon had little of that.

There was also the matter of the Mayday fair. There had been animals killed in the fields in recent times, cattle, and sheep, their remains mutilated. Simon had kept this news from Jessica. He trapped his lower lip between his teeth. So many secrets, so many lies. He could not hold them all forever.

The gossips in the tavern spoke of witchcraft and some fingers had pointed Jessica's way. If Jessica appeared at the fair, tongues loosened by ale and gin might accuse her. If she stayed home, those same tongues would accuse her anyway. Her presence risked the vengeance of an ale-fuelled mob. They would take her absence as guilt. Was she best hidden at his house, or in her own cottage? Should he take her away from here, to another town? Simon lacked the brain for such decisions. He needed help.

Simon hurried back along his poacher-paths, toward the windowless tower beside Lord West's mansion. Nicholas Demdike would tell him what to do.

Chapter Four

The patch of light on the floor edged closer to the mark that signaled midnight.

Jessica checked the door, made sure it was securely fastened then ran to her bed and pulled the books from beneath it. She placed the books on the table beside the rabbits Simon had left. Belson mewed at her, and pawed at the rabbits.

"What is it, Belson? I don't have time to feed you now." Jessica opened Goetia to the page that described the circle she needed to draw. Belson mewed again, and tapped her hand with his paw. He nudged the rabbits with his nose, then jumped off the table and ran to the door.

Jessica looked from the rabbits to Belson. "You want me to put them outside?" She lifted the rabbits; their hind legs still tied with Simon's twine, and took them to the door. "If I leave them out there, the rats and crows will eat them."

Belson mewed and clawed at the wooden frame. Jessica sighed and opened the door. Her mother had told her to trust Belson, so there must be a reason for all this. She looked around for a safe place to leave the rabbits, and then remembered the rusted iron hook protruding from the wall beside the door, just above head height. Jessica hung the rabbits from the hook.

"That's all the meat we have, Belson. What if it's gone in the morning?" Jessica considered the rabbits for a moment. She waved her hands over them, muttering a few words. The rabbits faded from sight. Jessica examined the space below the hook but even her witch-sight could discern no outline of rabbits, not so much as a ripple in the stone behind them. Satisfied, she stepped back into the house. Belson sat on the table, beside Goetia. Jessica closed the door and returned to the book.

"I've cast an invisibility spell over them. It won't stop rats smelling them though." Jessica checked the progress of the moonlight on the floor. Not much time left. She took two sticks from beside the fireplace, tied them with a length of sewing thread and walked to the middle of the floor. She pressed one stick into the ground, then, with the thread held taut, drew a large circle around it with the other.

Belson examined the circle as she scraped it into the floor. He watched every sigil, every line she drew. Sometimes he stopped her with his paw, when she made a mistake.

Finally, Jessica stood and stretched. Her circle was complete. Five tallow candles marked the circumference. Now she needed a triangle, outside the circle, big enough to hold the demon. Belson led her to where the moonlight approached her midnight mark, and Jessica scraped a hasty triangle in the floor around it.

"It's big enough for a man to stand in. I hope this Foras will appear as a man." Jessica shuddered, recalling some of the descriptions of the demons in Goetia. "Well, Belson, it's time." She picked up her mother's spell book, left Goetia on the table, and stood in the centre of the circle.

Shadows formed by the flickering candles danced on the cracked stone walls. Smoke curled upwards in the rising warmth, to escape through one of the larger holes in the thatched roof. The moonlight's beam became visible in the smoke-haze. Its illumination touched the midnight-mark.

Jessica read through the incantation she had used to call her mother's ghost, hoping it would work on a powerful demon as well as on a spirit. Satisfied that she knew it by heart, she took a deep breath and prepared to speak.

Her arms, spread wide, lifted the white gown to her knees. Belson joined her in the circle and sat at her bare feet, with his tail curled around her ankle. Smoke from the candles formed a spiral above them, their vapors swirling into a vortex.

Jessica nodded at the form of the spiral: it turned deosil, the direction of invocation. The smoke spun faster as Jessica spoke the first line of the incantation.

"I do invocate and conjure thee, O Spirit Foras, and being with power armed from the Supreme Majesty, I do strongly command thee, by *Beralanensis*, *Baldachiensis*, *Paumachia*, and *Apologiae Sedes*."

Jessica's voice rose and fell with the rhythm of the words. The smoke gathered within the shaft of moonlight. She held it there with her mind and voice while the beam moved, slowly, across the triangle.

"Also by the names *Adonai*, *El*, *Elohim*, *Elohi*, *Ehyeh Asher Ehyeh*, *Zabaoth*, *Elion*, *Iah*, *Tetragrammaton*."

The room grew cold as Jessica funneled all her energy into the smoke, using her mind to force its particles together to form a tenuous shape. The outline of a man, tall and broad, grew from the smoke and dust in the air. A pair of green eyes glowed in the wispy fabric of its head. The incantation completed, Jessica called the demon's name once more.

"Foras!"

Exhausted, Jessica let her shoulders slump and her head droop for a moment, before raising her face to see the result of her conjuration. Foras stared back, and the leaf-green luminosity of his eyes seemed to bore into her soul. He flexed his arms. The motion caused the dark green leather of his clothing to creak with the force of the muscles beneath. Jet-black hair flowed to his shoulders.

Jessica realized her mouth hung open and forced it closed. She had hoped for a man-like apparition, but Foras far exceeded her expectations. Images of some of the young men of the village, men she had admired, flashed through her mind. They were like gargoyles compared to the man—demon—standing in her triangle.

"You resemble Elizabeth Chadwick, you have Belson, her familiar, yet you are not her." The flawless skin on Foras's face creased in a smile.

Jessica took a deep breath. "I am Jessica Chadwick, daughter of Elizabeth. She is dead."

"Yes." Foras's gaze moved over her body. "I know of her death. I have spoken with her since. Many of your ancestors are known to me." He looked into her eyes. "What is it you wish, Jessica Chadwick? You must have something important in mind, to risk conversation with demons on this night."

"I have, great Foras. A task beyond anything I have attempted before."

"But not beyond your abilities, I hope?" Foras raised one eyebrow.

Jessica sighed. "I fear it might be. I will need help. A great deal of help."

Foras nodded. "Tell me. Then I will decide whether to give you this help."

Belson rubbed against Jessica's legs, diverting her attention for a moment. She glanced at the cat, long enough to see its nod of encouragement. Jessica took a deep breath and stared directly into Foras's eyes. "I wish to kill someone."

Foras sniffed. "Is that all? You have spells and herbs aplenty with which to complete so simple a task. You need no help from me." His face grew serious. "Are you becoming like your great-aunt, old Mother Chattox? Such thoughts and actions led her to the gallows, remember."

"That was before I was born, great Foras, and no, I will not succumb to her darkness. This killing will be for the good of many."

"I see." Foras rubbed his chin. "Then you wish to interfere in the war that rages in your land?"

"No. The war will run its own course. I wish only one death, but that one has already been responsible for the deaths of hundreds."

Foras smiled, an easy, superior expression. Jessica cleared her throat.

"I wish to kill the creature known as Matthew Hopkins, the Witchfinder."

The smile on Foras's lips grew into a grin, developed into a snigger and finally into roaring laughter.

Jessica's cheeks warmed as she watched the demon's mirth, but she dared not interrupt. Foras was powerful, and she needed him to complete her task. To antagonize him now would mean failure, and possibly worse. She waited in silence until his laughter subsided.

"This is no task for you, Jessica. You may kill the man, but that which is within him will move on. It has moved on before, countless times, and it will continue." He pursed his lips for a moment. "Your mother asked the same thing. Too late. It had already found her."

"I know." Jessica spoke through gritted teeth. She paused until her jaw relaxed before continuing. "Mother told me, but she gave no details."

"Then I will. This Unmade, the creature known to us as a Golab, is an ancient beast. It possessed the Inquisitor who tortured and burned your mother. It possessed the magistrate who sentenced your great-aunt and her friends, before that. Many others, down the ages, have fed its lust for fear. When the man dies, the Golab finds another."

"So now it is Matthew Hopkins?"

"Indeed." Foras ran his hand through his hair. "Killing him will be pointless. The Golab will endure."

Jessica stared at the floor for a moment. "So how can the Golab be destroyed?"

Foras's easy smile returned. "This Golab is a pet of Asmodeus, one of the great Kings of Hell. You have a quandary, my pretty Jessica. I, and those like me, cannot kill it without precipitating a war. One which would make your battles here look like schoolroom squabbles. A war which would encompass the Earth and lay waste to all life." Foras grew in stature as he spoke, until he towered over Jessica. The room darkened as though a cloud covered the moon.

Jessica shivered, but held her voice steady. "Then I must kill it."

"You cannot. The paradox of the Golab is that it can only be killed by human hand, yet the power of a demon is needed to dispel its life."

"So it can never be killed?"

"That is not what I said." Foras resumed his normal size, a little over six feet tall. The green in his eyes flashed with his smile.

Jessica considered this. She needed the power of a demon, but the hand of a human. She stepped forward, to the edge of the circle, to stand within a few feet of Foras.

"Possess me, then. Come into me, Foras. Use my hands, and your power, and we can be rid of this thing."

Foras shook his head, still smiling. "It is not so easy, sweet witch. The human must be unaware of the demon within. The demon cannot control the human, or there will be war. It is a delicate thing, and will take time to arrange."

"How much time?"

Foras grinned. "We have considered this matter, the others and I, since the time your mother asked it of us. We have identified a family who will eventually produce a suitable host. One who can be possessed without knowing. The demon must not affect its host in any way. No guidance can come from within, and little from without. The host must eventually meet the Golab, and fight it. Then, and only then, can the demon within pass its power to the host, and allow him to kill the creature."

"How long will it take?" Jessica winced at the impatience in her tone.

"To arrange such a thing will take at least three centuries."

Jessica sank to her knees, defeated. "Then it is hopeless. In three centuries, the Golab will have killed thousands."

"Unless it is trapped." Foras inspected his fingernails, watching Jessica with a sidelong look.

"Trapped." Jessica closed her eyes. If the thing was rendered harmless, if it could be contained for three centuries or more, until the demon/human hybrid could be made...

She surged to her feet. "How can it be trapped?"

Foras roared with laughter. "My pretty witch has an adventure in mind, I see. Fortunately, your wishes coincide with those of my brothers and me. You are aware of our state? Have your researches extended so far?"

Bowing her head, Jessica stared at her hands. She spoke in a quiet voice. "You were once Angels, but fell from Grace. I know not why, nor what it is you seek."

"No matter. Enough to say that some of us will help you in this quest, and willingly. We will build a trap for this Golab, and assist you in the preparations you need to make for the future, three centuries hence."

Jessica looked up, suddenly worried. "You said 'we'. How many demons must I call? What price will they ask of me?"

Foras stared at Belson, who had left the circle and now stood within the triangle with Foras. He returned his gaze to Jessica. "Belson tells me you have the Goetia."

An involuntary turn of her head brought Jessica's gaze briefly to the book on the table against the far wall, behind her. "I have. I stole it from the monastery, while my friend distracted the monks."

"Oh?" Concern creased Foras's brow. "There is another who knows of this?"

"No, he doesn't know I took the book. I only told him I wanted to see the monks' library."

"Good. We will have to hurry, before Asmodeus learns of our intentions. He will try to stop us. Now, fetch the Goetia here."

The command in his tone sent Jessica hurrying across the room. She stopped at the edge of the circle and looked back at Foras.

"I cannot leave the circle, or you will take my soul. Has this all been a trick, Foras?"

"No harm will come to you. This I promise." Foras held up both hands. Belson crossed the circle to stand beside Jessica. He purred as he rubbed against her legs.

"Is it true, Belson?" she whispered. "Will I be safe or damned?" The book was out of reach, she had no option but to leave the circle to get it. If Foras was lying, the moment she stepped from the circle she would die, and her soul would join the legions of Hell.

Jessica blinked a tear from her eye. If she refused, then she gave up all hope of defeating the Golab. The Witchfinder would kill her, and the Golab would continue its killing spree. There was nothing to lose. Jessica took a deep breath and stepped from the circle.

As she picked up Goetia, the room filled with a green light. The candles extinguished while the fire flared into brilliance. Jessica hugged the book to her chest, not daring to turn around.

"Oh, I must have forgotten to mention this." Foras's voice, close to her ear, made her shriek. The Goetia fell from her hands and she turned, trembling, to look up into those luminous eyes.

Foras grinned. "When you left the circle, you broke its power. I am free to walk your world now."

Chapter Five

Simon left the path in silence at the sound of footsteps. The heavy tread suggested soldiers, and soldiers were not to be trusted out here in the woods. Besides, he still carried a hare and two rabbits on his belt. That was enough to get him arrested. The soldiers would certainly take them from him, whether they arrested him or not. He squatted behind a bush, close to a willow tree that provided shade from the revealing moonlight.

Three soldiers passed on the narrow path, heading toward Lord West's mansion. Simon held his breath as he listened to their conversation, their words slurred with Marchway ale.

"You think he will pay?"

"Better than our own Parliament, at least."

Drunken laughter cut the night. One of the men paused, and called to his fellows to wait. He stumbled from the path toward the bush where Simon sat, fumbled with his trousers, and then urinated at the bush. Splashes of the hot liquid flew between the budding branches, dampening Simon's clothes. A few warm drops hit Simon's face. He wrinkled his nose in disgust but dared not move. Trying to ignore the indignity, Simon concentrated on the conversation between the men.

"That Hopkins gets well paid for it."

"Then we should demand the same. It's the same job."

"You're sure there's one here? In this village?"

"Certain. The monks think she stole one of their books. A magical grimoire."

"That would be proof enough, if she has it."

"What was that name they said? Chatton?"

The soldier finished his toilet and pulled his clothes together before turning back to his friends. "Chadwick. The monks have been watching her for some time now. They say her mother was burned at the stake."

"They are sure the daughter is a witch also?"

The men resumed walking, their backs to Simon. He took the opportunity to move away from the dripping bush. One last remark came to him as the soldiers faded into the night.

"Does it matter? We'll get paid, just the same."

Their laughter rang in Simon's ears. Jessica must have stolen a book from the monastery, the time she had accompanied him on one of his visits. She had wanted him to distract the monks so she could look at their library, a task he found all too easy with a belly full of the monks' ale.

If the monks knew of Elizabeth, and suspected Jessica of witchcraft, then she was in grave danger. In these times, the slightest suspicion of witchcraft could get a woman burned or hanged.

He stood and leaned on the willow until he was sure the soldiers had gone. Then he ran back toward Jessica's house.

Chapter Six

Jessica clung to the stone wall. Its cold at her back served as a reminder of reality. Her knees shook, her legs threatened to collapse under her at any moment.

Foras bent down and retrieved Goetia from the floor. "You are right to quake in fear. Had you called Paimon, or Astaroth, or any one of a dozen others, you would now be shredded, a soft decoration for the walls of this room. Your soul would scream in Hell for all eternity." He placed the book on the table. "However, your quest interests me, as it will interest others. You need not fear. I have said I will not harm you."

Jessica whimpered and tried to press herself through the wall as Foras moved toward her. Her hands moved in an attempt to form the invisibility spell she had performed on the rabbits, but her voice refused to produce the words of the incantation.

Foras reached out and brushed a tear from her cheek. His touch warmed her, without the burning she had expected. Blinking, she stared as Foras raised his fingers to his eyes and examined the moisture on them.

"It is a mystery, this leakage from the face." He shook his head. "What purpose does it serve? When you are in danger, you blur your vision with water. Yet if you did not, you could see the danger for what it often is." He rubbed his fingers together and turned his eyes to hers. "Illusion."

"You are an illusion?" Jessica gasped the words, fighting to breathe through her terror.

"I am not."

"Then the danger is real."

"There is real danger, yes, but the danger is not me." Foras regarded the door. "If I am not mistaken, something dangerous to you is coming this way." He lifted the book and stepped into the circle. "We must hurry. Join me in the circle, and control your fear. It will not help you now."

Forcing herself away from the wall, Jessica noticed her circle. It was black, burned into the floor of the room along with the symbols it contained. She groaned. This evidence was permanent, visible to all who entered her cottage. If anyone saw it, she would hang for certain.

Jessica took a series of deep breaths to still the turmoil in her mind. There was no going back. She had to trust in Foras, had to continue her intended course. Standing in the circle, his back to her, Foras turned the pages of Goetia. Jessica wondered if the course she was on was indeed her own.

With an effort, she moved her unsteady legs until she stood beside Foras. Belson joined her. He rubbed his warm, comforting fur against her shins and mewed his encouragement.

Foras snapped his fingers and the candles re-ignited. Jessica sniffed the air. There was no acrid tallow stench, the candles gave off an aroma like herbs, like dew-fresh grass, pine and oak, the scents of woodland and growing things. Calm, peaceful thoughts filled her mind as Foras opened the Goetia and began to read. He sketched a symbol in the air. It hung in green fire, suspended by some invisible force.

Green filled the burnt lines of her circle, which glowed as bright as the candlelight. Jessica strained to follow the words Foras spoke, but his speech was too fast. She caught only the last word, as a dark, strange form materialized within the triangle.

"Malphas."

Jessica closed her eyes, then opened them. A crow stood within the triangle, regarding Foras and herself with black, gleaming eyes. An unremarkable manifestation, except that the crow was five feet tall, with wings that ended in feathered hands. One of the hands clutched a large trowel. Jessica turned to Foras, forming her question with her eyes.

Foras ignored her and moved forward. "The circle calls, but cannot hold us, Malphas. You may walk freely here."

Stepping from the triangle, Malphas moved to the nearest wall. "A crude construction, but serviceable." He looked down. "Dear me. The floor is nothing more than dirt. Why, the ancients built with more care than this." He turned his beady eyes on Jessica. "Have you people forgotten how to build?"

"We have more important matters to consider." There was a chuckle in Foras's voice. "Malphas, do you recall our discussions?"

The feathered head tilted to one side. "We have discussed many things, Foras."

"I mean our discussions concerning the Unmade."

"Oh, that." Malphas crossed the room to stand directly before Foras and Jessica. "You are referring to the destruction of the

Unmade, and how such an act would be of value to our cause?"

"Yes."

Malphas raised his feathers, and then lowered them, an action that may have been a shrug. "What of it? We decided it could not be done. Not without precipitating conflict on an appalling scale."

Foras nodded toward Jessica. "It can be done, Malphas."

"With this witch?" Malphas scratched his head with his trowel and hopped closer to Jessica. "She will not live to see it happen. How could this action benefit her?"

The foot-long black beak hovered inches from Jessica's face. She swallowed, cleared her throat, and looked directly into the eyes of this new demon. "This Golab is in a man called Matthew Hopkins. He kills witches and innocents alike. I want to stop him."

"Indeed?" Malphas clacked his beak. "Foras, have you told her how long this will take?"

"He has." Jessica squared her shoulders, determined to show no fear. "Three hundred years. Our first act must be to trap this monster until such time as you are ready."

Malphas turned away, tapping his beak. "I don't know. Construction of a suitable trap would present little difficulty, but it must stay hidden for three centuries or more. There is also the small matter of Asmodeus." He dug his trowel into the dirt floor and marked out a large square. "He won't like it."

"You can build such a trap, then?" Foras folded his arms.

"I can, yes. Can you hide it?"

"No. There are others who can, though."

"There are few of us left, Foras. How many can we be sure of?" The square complete, Malphas waved his trowel over it, muttering. The ground cracked and heaved within the square.

"Enough, I think. Malphas, we have this chance. We must try."

A perfectly smooth flagstone lifted from the dirt, its edges trimmed and dressed. Jessica's mouth fell open. Malphas sniffed as he considered his work. Jessica looked up at Foras, who smiled and winked at her.

Malphas wandered to the wall and tapped it with his trowel. "This will not do. I will need much more space."

"Take the space, Malphas. Use the woods outside. Mould, blend and shape as you will. The whole will be hidden." Foras opened Goetia. "I will call the others." He looked at Jessica. "We can make the trap, but we cannot bring the Golab here. That will be up to you."

"Oh, so there is some part for me in this?" Petulance surfaced in Jessica's mind, bringing her courage mingled with indignation. She had summoned Foras, she should be in command of this situation. Her breath caught as she realized just how quickly she had lost control. Her mother was right. Jessica was meddling with forces beyond her comprehension. Foras had brushed her aside as though she were a child.

"Understand." Foras leaned forward, his face close enough to hers that she could feel the warmth within it. "Your part is vital. We can build the trap, we can ensnare this Golab. We cannot bring it here. Our path is a thin line now; we must walk it with great care. Anything we do that could be seen as directly influencing events here might draw the attention of others of our kind. If Asmodeus finds us interfering, he will rise up, and there will be war."

"So I must entice the creature to come here? How will I do that?" Jessica half-closed her eyes and basked in the warmth and the cinnamon breath of Foras.

"I fear you will find it all too easy." Foras drew back, his smile tight. "The means is on its way here as we speak."

A sharp rap at the door interrupted Jessica's response. She looked from Foras to Malphas, both of whom stared at the door. Malphas surrounded himself with a gray haze. His body reduced in size until he appeared to be an ordinary crow. He flew to the largest hole in the roof and perched on its edge, looking down.

"We must not be seen, not yet. Remember, we cannot interfere in the normal lives of others." Foras retreated against the wall and blended with it. Jessica could make out his shape if she concentrated, but it was unlikely anyone else could see him.

The rap at the door sounded again. A muffled voice, low and urgent, came through the wood. "Jessica. It's Simon. I have to speak to you."

Jessica groaned. What could the old poacher want now? She removed the bar from the door and opened it, just enough to show Simon her face.

"What is it, Simon? It's late, I have to sleep."

"I'm sorry, Jessica. I wouldn't have come, but it's very important." Simon was panting, his brow slick with sweat. "I saw soldiers on the path, heading toward Lord West's mansion."

"Well, they won't come here, then." Jessica shrugged. "You could have told me of this tomorrow."

"They mentioned your name."

"Me?"

"They say the monks have named you as a witch. They intend to claim a bounty for pointing you out."

Jessica forced a laugh, aware that the cracking of her voice betrayed her nervousness. "There is nothing to worry about, Simon. I have harmed nobody."

Simon shook his head. "It doesn't matter. They will name you and claim the bounty anyway. Jessica, you know that many of those hanged as witches were innocent. Even the Church has spoken against the Witchfinder these past months. Innocent or not, it makes no difference. The soldiers have no money and they are desperate. They will take what they can get."

He paused to glance back along the path as though afraid he might have been followed. "I can hide you. Take what you can carry, and come with me. Please, Jessica. I don't want the soldiers to hang you."

"Don't worry, Simon. I will be safe here tonight. Nothing will happen before tomorrow." Jessica wished she felt as confident as she sounded. Part of her wanted to leave with Simon, to take her chances in hiding, but that might be seen as an admission of guilt.

Besides, she could hardly leave her house in the care of two demons, neither of whom she entirely trusted. Foras still held the Goetia. With that, he could call another seventy demons, and each of them could call legions of spirits. No, she had to stay, even though her chances of controlling Foras were slim. She had summoned him. It would be irresponsible to walk away and leave him to his own devices.

"If you will not come, then I will wait along the path. If I see anyone, I will run to warn you." Simon stuck out his chin.

"Oh no, Simon. You don't have to do that. Go home, sleep, I will be here tomorrow."

Simon blew a long, drawn-out sigh. "I must do something. Goodnight, Jessica. With luck, Lord West will pay these men no heed." He looked into her eyes. "If the Witchfinder hears, it will be another matter."

Jessica shivered. The Witchfinder would have to hear, sooner or later. She needed him to come here, but not too soon. Not before the demons had constructed their prison.

"Well, goodnight, Simon. We can speak again tomorrow." She closed the door, ignoring Simon's continuing protests, and slid the wooden bar into place. Jessica leaned her head against the door, her eyes closed.

Foras had told her something dangerous was coming. He said

the means to summon the Witchfinder was at her door. Simon? No, he had been a trusted friend since she was a child. Foras must have been talking about the soldiers who were to accuse her. How long did she have? She straightened and turned to face Foras, who had resumed his place in the circle.

"Foras, wait. I have questions." She started toward him but her movement stalled. Jessica stared in disbelief. The entire rear wall of her house had vanished. "What have you done?"

Where there should have been solid stone, a feathery network of silver lines supported the roof, allowing the night air to drift throughout her simple cottage. Her herb garden, behind the house, had been replaced by a large area of flagstones. A new wall was forming, at the far edge of these stones, attended by a black blur that must have been Malphas. Jessica turned her gaze to Foras, to his infuriating smile.

"Malphas said he needed more space. Trust him, he is a good builder. Your house will be the better for his work." Foras opened Goetia and ran his finger along a page.

"My garden—"

"There will be a new garden. Malphas will form it, I will plant it, and others will hide it."

Jessica clamped her head between her hands, fingers knotted in her hair. "Foras, people will notice. You can't just turn a cottage into a mansion, overnight. They already suspect me of witchcraft. This will be more proof than anyone could need."

Foras shrugged. "Good."

"Good?" Tears welled in Jessica's eyes. "They will hang me."

"You wish to bring the Golab here? This Matthew Hopkins will not come unless someone accuses you of witchcraft." Green light burned in Foras's eyes, sufficient to illuminate the book in his hands. "Now, if you will remain silent, I will continue the calling. There is much to do."

Her vision blurred, Jessica stumbled to her simple wooden bed and sat down. She wiped her eyes on her sleeve and stared in resentment at Foras's back. Behind her, where there should have been a wall, were the clacking sounds of bricks being laid. Jessica turned her head, amazed at the speed with which Malphas worked. He seemed to pull the stones from the air, his trowel never free of mortar. The wall grew as she watched, layer after layer.

Fatigued by the effort of her recent conjurations, Jessica lay on the bed and glared at Foras. This was her house, her circle, her magic. Now she had lost everything. She was nothing more than a plaything in the hands of these demons. Bait for their trap.

Perhaps she should have left with Simon. There was nothing she could do here, nothing but wait and hope the demon's trap was completed in time. Belson jumped onto the bed and curled beside her, purring. Jessica stroked his fur. Battling the weights that tugged at her eyelids, she watched Foras reach the end of another incantation. Once more, she caught only the final word.

"Orobas."

A magnificent white horse appeared in the triangle. Its form contorted and shrank while it raised itself on its hind legs. Jessica tried to focus through tired eyes, to see what the horse would become, but the image blended with her dreams as she drifted into sleep.

Chapter Seven

Simon ran to the tower beside Lord West's mansion. Stone gargoyles leered down at him from the gloom, their features stark and alive with the glow of the moon. He reached for the brass knocker and hammered it, three times then two, then three again. Simon stepped back. His sides ached with the exertion of running here, and the cold air burned his throat.

The door swung inwards with a creak of iron hinges. Simon shook himself and stepped inside, knowing what to expect.

Nobody greeted him, nobody asked his business, and nobody questioned his arrival so late at night. Those who called at this hour either had urgent business or had lost all reason. Simon took a deep breath and called out.

"Master Demdike. It is Simon Bulcock, with news. Important news." Deep breaths spaced the words. Simon fought to bring his breathing under control.

"I know who you are, Simon. We're old friends, aren't we?"

The calm, quiet voice came from the shadows in one of the alcoves. Simon shuddered as Nicholas Demdike moved into the light. Demdike's black robes brushed the ground and his monk's cowl obscured the upper part of his face.

He crossed the smooth black floor, although Simon could never discern the movement of his legs, until he was within a foot of Simon's face. Demdike towered over him, a gaunt though imposing figure that always reminded Simon of the images of Death he had seen at the monastery in Marchway.

"Soldiers." Simon stammered, struggling to breathe between phrases. "Coming here. Jessica. They know."

"Ah, Simon." Demdike moved to Simon's side and put one arm around his shoulders, propelling him toward a door at the far end of the hallway. "Calm yourself. The rational mind controls events, the emotional mind is controlled by events. Have you forgotten your lessons? Dispel your emotion, and then tell me your news."

Simon took several deep breaths. Nicholas had explained this before. In order to control magic, Simon had to learn to control himself. They stopped at the door.

"I went to see Jessica."

"Yes, you were to warn her of the soldiers camped at Marchway. You were also taking her a brace of rabbits, as I recall?"

"Yes. I—"

"And did you deliver the rabbits?" Demdike released Simon's shoulder and stood to one side of the door.

"I did." Simon shot a puzzled glance at his mentor.

"She accepted them? You left them in the house?"

"Yes, but—"

"Inside the house?" Demdike steepled his fingers. His head bowed so that the hood now covered all of his face.

"Yes. What does it matter?"

"Small things matter, Simon. Now, continue with your news."

"There was a perfume in the air. I recognized it. Elizabeth's perfume. The scent of her herbs." The room took on an unexpected chill. Simon pulled his coat around himself.

"Elizabeth." Demdike raised his head, showing a thin-lipped smile. "So Jessica has achieved her potential, and spoken with her mother. Did you see the spirit with your own eyes?"

"No, and it is just as well. Elizabeth might know how she came to be accused. The dead know of things we try to hide." Simon hung his head. "It seems I was lucky she did not tell Jessica."

"Ah, Simon, all that is in the past, you must let it go." Demdike waited until Simon looked up before continuing. "I know your concern is for Jessica, as is mine. Do not assume Elizabeth will accuse you. The dead know many things, yes, but they are not omnipotent. It is possible to hide from them."

Demdike pursed his cracked lips. "Now, since you were in the house immediately after the manifestation, you can help me to understand her method. Describe the markings on her floor."

Simon shook his head. "There were no markings. The floor was the same as always."

"Really? No circle? No symbols?" Demdike rubbed his chin with his bony fingers. "She takes chances, this one. I think it's time I took her under my wing, so to speak. Calling spirits without protection is a terrible risk. It's time she learned to use her powers properly."

"Yes, Master Demdike." Simon breathed a sigh of relief. Once Jessica was in Nicholas's care, she would be safe from soldiers, witchfinders, and angry villagers. "There were soldiers also."

"Yes, I know about them." Demdike took hold of the door handle.

"No, not just at Marchway. Three of them are coming to see Lord West. They intend to accuse Jessica of witchcraft. She would not leave with me. She might listen to you. We should take her from the house tonight."

"There is no need for such unseemly haste, Simon. We can wait until morning. The rabbits you left will protect her from her own magic. With dead meat in the room, no spirit will answer her call." Demdike chuckled. "Well, no spirit she's likely to want to call will answer." He turned the handle.

"The soldiers, Master Demdike. We must prevent them accusing her."

"As I said, I know of them. I saw them coming, and met them on the road." Demdike pushed the door open. A charnel-house stench flooded the hallway. "We can't have anyone else interfering with our Jessica, now can we?"

Simon constricted his throat to quell the nausea rising from his stomach. Within the room were three figures. Stripped of armor, clothes and skin, they hung on the wall as though crucified. A bowl below each one collected the blood that dripped from multiple lacerations in their flesh.

One of the men stirred. His skinless head rolled on his shoulders. Peeled, dry eyes stared at Simon, blood streamed between lipless teeth as the soldier produced a series of gurgling sounds.

Simon turned his face from the sight and spoke to Demdike. "He's trying to say something."

Demdike's breath whistled in his throat. "Their time for speaking has passed." He indicated a stone shelf set into the wall beside the door.

In an instant, Simon's desire for magical abilities fled. If it meant he would have to do this—

He clutched at his stomach and stumbled back into the hallway, the image seared into the backs of his eyes. The stone shelf bore a single, upright iron spike. Pierced on that spike were three pieces of flesh, pieces Simon recognized.

Tongues.

Chapter Eight

"Wake up, Jessica."

Jessica groaned. She wanted the voice to go away and let her sleep. When it spoke again, she buried her face in her straw-filled mattress.

"Wake up. It's morning."

The voice was sweet and melodic, not like the earthy tones of Foras or the hoarse croak of Malphas. The memory of the previous night brought her fully awake. Jessica opened her eyes and pulled back her blanket to stare at the speaker.

It was a small boy, no more than ten or eleven years old, although his golden eyes held many more years than his slight frame could have seen. Red hair, the same color as hers, fell across his shoulders. He was dressed in a simple white robe, much like the one Jessica wore. Radiance, gold and fiery, surrounded him. Jessica sat up.

"Who are you?"

"I am Phenex. Pleased to make your acquaintance, Jessica Chadwick." Phenex held out his hand. "Foras has explained how you will help us."

"How I will help you? I called Foras to help me."

"It's the same thing, in the end. Helping you will be of benefit to us." Phenex withdrew his hand. "You know we tried once before, with Solomon? It didn't work as we had planned. This time, we hope to do better."

"You're a demon?"

"I prefer the term 'fallen', although 'demon' will do." Phenex grinned, showing perfect teeth.

Jessica sat up, rubbing her eyes, and yelped when her feet touched cold stone. She looked down to see an ornate, multicolored tiled floor. Raising her head brought a wooden staircase into view, traveling upwards to where there should have been no upper floor.

"What has Malphas done?" Throwing her blankets aside, Jessica stood and surveyed what her small cottage had become. The loosely-fixed planks of her front door had been replaced with solid, paneled and polished wood. The beam she used to lock the door was gone, the door now sported a brass handle and lock plate along with wrought iron hinges. The walls were smooth and straight. They were paneled in oak halfway up, the rest painted a delicate blue.

Above her head, a white ceiling sported plaster moldings along its edges; a silver and glass chandelier, filled with candles, hung from the centre. In the wall to the left of the front door, where there should have been nothing but bare stone, was another polished door, and yet another was set into the side of the staircase. Of her fireplace there was no sign.

"My God." Jessica's hand covered her mouth. "This is too much to hide. Even Lord West will be envious."

"Malphas works well, does he not?" The child who called himself Phenex stood beside her. "Oh, and we prefer not to be noticed. If you could avoid invoking the Almighty just yet, it would be appreciated." Phenex took her hand and tugged. "Come, there is much to see."

Dazed, Jessica allowed Phenex to lead her past the staircase, toward the newly formed wall at the back of the house. An opening led into a corridor with a door to her left and another to her right. Phenex opened the door on the right.

"Kitchen." He smiled up at her. Jessica stared, unable to grasp the sight. The room was filled with iron and copper utensils—pots and pans like those she had seen at market but never dreamed she would ever own. A large fire burned in a fireplace in the far wall, a selection of spits racked beside it. She had no time to take in the full impact of the room before Phenex closed the door. He pulled her across the corridor to the opposite door and pushed it open.

A long corridor stretched before them, curving to the right, its right-hand wall made up of enormous windows. Through these windows, the curve of the building showed until it vanished into the woods.

Jessica traced her fingers over the glass. She had never seen such large panes before. There seemed to be no means to open these windows. They were fixed into hardwood frames that ran floor to ceiling, with slender pillars set between them.

Jessica sagged, her head lowered and shaking. "This is not my house. You have taken me somewhere else."

Phenex laughed, a tinkle like thin glass breaking. "This is yours, Jessica. This is the opening of our trap."

There was movement in the woods outside. Trees seemed to

be shrinking, walking around. Jessica blinked and stared down at Phenex. She had never imagined magic on this scale, never considered such power could even exist. For a moment, Jessica wondered what she had unleashed on the world. One thing was certain, she had no hope of controlling the demons now. She mouthed a silent prayer. *Mother, what have I done?*

"Where does the corridor go?" Jessica could hear defeat and resignation in her own voice.

"This is the circle. The trap will be within." Phenex grinned up at her. "It has to hold a Golab, remember. Your little circle was just a play-pen for small magic. We need something much bigger to contain the power you wish to ensnare."

"So this corridor is one big circle?" Jessica stared along the glass wall. "How big?"

"One thousand yards in diameter. The triangle will be within the house. We don't really need it, but Malphas insisted. He won't do slipshod work, he says."

A scurrying in the long grass outside interrupted Jessica's amazement. Something moved, fast and low, leaving a channel in its wake. She strained her eyes but could not make out its shape.

"That will be Bifrons." Phenex's eyes glittered with some secret amusement. "I don't think you're ready to meet Bifrons."

"How many?" Jessica shook her head. "Has Foras called them all? Are the seventy-two demons of the Goetia running loose in these woods?" Jessica stared at Phenex, whose face became serious.

"Ah, only twelve of us remain. The rest fell back to the darkness after we were freed from Solomon's prison. Not all at once, but gradually, they turned their faces from the light and gave up hope."

Phenex turned and walked toward the door, his hands behind his back. "Twelve of us remain, still hoping to perform sufficient penitence to be allowed back into the Host." He looked over his shoulder at Jessica. "Come, I have more to show you."

Jessica followed, her mind reeling. These demons hoped to return to Heaven, to make amends for the actions that led to them being cast down. The entrapment and eventual demise of the Golab may go some way to achieving their aims. She allowed Phenex to lead her to the staircase, where a small door was set in its side. He pulled the door open.

A flight of stairs led down into darkness. Phenex walked down a few steps, his aura brightening to fill the stairwell with a golden radiance. He smiled up at her.

"Follow me, and we shall inspect the progress of our trap."

Chapter Nine

Light blue filled the early sky by the time Simon left Nicholas Demdike's tower. Fatigue dulled his senses and slowed his movements. Nicholas had given him instructions, to be completed with urgency. The soldiers would be missed and neither Simon nor Nicholas knew whether they had told any of their fellows where they were going. Nicholas had questioned them but had learned nothing. Simon knew, too well, what form that questioning had taken. The sight had dispelled his ambition to learn magic; all he cared about now was Jessica.

The village, and his home, lay to his left. Simon turned right, toward Jessica's cottage. He had to be sure she was safe, and still there. His warnings may have caused her to flee, and Nicholas could not protect her if she ran away.

Stumbling along the path, Simon took no care to move without sound. This was daylight, requiring none of the cautions of his nocturnal activities. He would check on Jessica, then go home and sleep for a few hours. Nicholas wanted his errand completed with haste, but Simon would never succeed without some sleep. He grinned. The Witchfinder would test Jessica, and Nicholas would see to it that she passed his tests. Then Jessica need have no fear of accusation.

"Well, well. Simon Bulcock. Late home after a night's poaching, I see."

Simon gasped as the man who had spoken behind him laid a heavy hand on his shoulder. He turned his head and met the leering face of Daniel Featherstone, bailiff for Lord West's land. Dressed in his bright red jerkin, his yellow sash of office around his waist, Daniel was normally easy to spot and avoid. Simon cursed himself for taking so little care this morning, but his mind had been distracted.

"I'm not poaching, Dan. Just walking." Simon struggled free of Daniel's grip and stood facing him. Running was pointless; Simon was too tired to flee even the flabby Daniel. The hare and rabbits at his belt pressed against his leg. Simon pulled his coat tighter around himself, feigning cold.

Jessica's Trap

"What would you be doing at this hour, if not poaching?" Hands on hips, Daniel glared at Simon. Daniel's face contorted in disgust. "You stink. Have you wet yourself?"

"No, I have not. I'm on an errand, for Lord West's adviser, Nicholas Demdike." Striving to appear important, Simon drew himself up to his full height, a few inches short of Daniel, who spat at the ground.

"Demdike. That evil old warlock. What are you thinking, associating with the likes of him? There is talk of witchcraft in the village, and Demdike is one of the names on people's tongues."

Simon winced. He would have preferred if Daniel had not mentioned tongues. Simon decided to bluff his way out of the conversation.

"You believe all that talk, Dan? A grown man, falling for tales of sprites and hobgoblins?"

Daniel laughed. "The church tells us witches are real, and should not be allowed to live. You would know that, if you visited the church once in a while." Daniel narrowed his eyes. "Although since you spend so much time with Demdike, and that so-called niece of yours, maybe you're a witch yourself." He looked down at Simon's coat, then reached forward and pulled it open. "Rabbits, and a hare. I've caught you poaching at last."

Simon tried to run, but Daniel overtook him in a few strides and wrenched Simon's arm around to pin it high on his back.

"You're coming with me, Simon Bulcock. There's a certain lord who would like a word with you."

"No, I have to go. Master Demdike expects his errand completed today. Take the rabbits, but let me go."

"It's prison for you, I think, and perhaps a little torture. I believe you know much more about our devil-worshipper than you admit." He twisted Simon's arm. "Who is it, Simon? Who's the witch?"

Simon gasped as pain lanced through his shoulder. He recalled a night in a tavern, in another town, long ago. Too much ale, too much free talk. Someone had asked him the same question and he had replied. The memory was vague and uncertain, but it haunted his thoughts still. His ale-loosened tongue had sent Jessica's mother to the fire. Matthew Chadwick, Jessica's father, had blamed Demdike for the betrayal, and Simon had never found the courage to admit it was his fault.

Simon bit his lip. The methods of the torturer had come to his ears as rumor, as late-night gossip over tankards of ale. If there were any truth in those tales, he would be better to die now. He could not betray Jessica, yet he doubted his ability to withstand the things he had heard described.

Another bolt of pain shot through him as Daniel twisted harder. Simon imagined Jessica in the hands of this bully, and determined to keep silent. Daniel, and those like him, would drag Jessica from her home and hang her before Nicholas could prevent it.

"I don't know, Dan. Do you think Demdike would tell me if he were a sorcerer? I might just run off and tell the Witchfinder, and claim the bounty for myself."

The pressure on his arm relaxed. Daniel grunted. "True. You are an untrustworthy rogue. Demdike, for all his devil-worship, is no fool."

Simon was almost lifted from the ground by the speed with which Daniel turned him around. He propelled him in the direction of Lord West's mansion. Although Simon offered no resistance, Daniel held his arm with more force than was necessary.

"Maybe I'll just tell your story to Lord West, and let him pry the truth from your precious Demdike." Daniel laughed as he pushed Simon faster.

Chapter Ten

The cellar was cold, but not damp. Jessica gaped at the granite blocks of the walls, the smooth stones of the floor.

"Malphas did this all while I slept? I must have been asleep for days."

"A few hours only. Malphas wastes no time." Phenex led her behind the stairs, his light casting her shadow in stark relief on the walls. He spoke a few words and a section of wall detached from the smooth brickwork and swung open. Grinning, he motioned for her to follow.

The tunnel was long and claustrophobic. Jessica hunched low, although there was ample room to stand. The weight of the ground above seemed to oppress her soul. She hugged herself for warmth, wishing she had put on more than the simple robe she had worn the night before.

How far away that time seemed now, how remote and alien. Her one-roomed cottage had been transformed into a warren of rooms and tunnels, filled with demons who should be tearing her apart, yet acted as though they were lifelong friends.

As she followed Phenex, Jessica wondered again what she had set in motion with her summoning of Foras. She noticed the iron sconces, each set with a yellow beeswax candle, along the walls. None were lit. The light Phenex produced was sufficient.

"Here we are." The tunnel ended in a plain brick wall. Phenex pronounced another spell and the wall opened as before. He took Jessica's hand and led her through.

The room within was a vast circular space with twelve thick, curved stone pillars supporting a domed ceiling. Each pillar bore a carved head. Foras, Malphas and Phenex were represented, so the other faces must belong to the remaining demons.

Jessica stared in amazement at the stonework, illuminated by more than just the brilliance of Phenex. Fire raged in a circle, contained within a trough set into the floor. Within this, in the centre of the room, was a device shaped like a bowl with an identical, though reversed, structure, in the ceiling directly above. Phenex laughed his breaking-glass laugh once again.

"See, our containment is almost ready. The pentacle above will be completed before the day is out, and we can capture the Golab whenever you bring it here."

Jessica sank to her knees, buried her face in her hands and wept.

"What is this? Are you displeased with our work?"

"No." Jessica choked through her sobs. "It is perfect. Wonderful. I had no idea. This is too much for me, too fast. I thought Foras would help me kill the Golab within the Witchfinder, but this..."

Phenex's small hand touched her shoulder. "Is something wrong?"

"It's too much." Jessica looked up, staring through her tears at the concern on Phenex's face. "I don't know how to bring the Witchfinder here. I never thought it would be this way. I thought Foras would tell me how to kill him. All these preparations. All this work. I don't know what to do."

"Foras has not told you?"

"I haven't spoken to Foras since last night, when I called him here. When he took over my circle, my house, my life."

"Ah, of course. Events have moved somewhat more rapidly than human comprehension allows. I will lead you back to Foras. He will explain." Phenex took her hand again and led her back into the tunnel, toward her new cellar.

They had moved perhaps twenty yards along the tunnel when a grating sound made Jessica turn. The door closed behind them, although Phenex had uttered no spell.

"Both doors will close themselves, if left unattended." Phenex spoke without breaking stride. "A precaution, to keep our trap hidden."

"What about my house? How will you hide that?"

"You will see, in due course. First we should speak with Foras."

Chapter Eleven

Simon collided with the wall beside the servant's entrance to Lord West's mansion. When Daniel released his arm, Simon slid down the wall, exhausted, finally coming to rest with his head against the cool stone. A dull ache remained in his right arm where Daniel had held him. Daniel rapped on the door and waited.

Through a tired haze, Simon heard the door open. Daniel's strident voice hurt his ears.

"I have to see Lord West. I have a poacher for him, and news."

Simon groaned as Daniel hauled him to his feet. He faced the servant who had answered the door. A small, thin man, dressed in crisp linen, a stark contrast to Simon's own clothing. Never the best, and worse now for his night of wandering, his brown woolen garments stuck to his skin. Breathing heavily, he tried to look the servant in the eye.

"Lord West is at breakfast." The servant's tone, and the look on his face, suggested he had no intention of interrupting his Lordship at his meal.

"We will wait." Daniel pushed Simon toward the door.

"Not in the kitchen. Not with that stink." The servant drew back to avoid colliding with Simon. "You can wait out here. I'll call you when His Lordship will see you." The servant closed the door, cutting off Daniel's protests. Daniel pushed Simon to the ground.

"Now see what you've got me into. Not even allowed into the house."

Simon grunted as Daniel kicked him in the ribs, and rolled to rest against the wall. His eyes closed, he wanted nothing more than sleep.

"I'm going to sit where I can see you, and have a pipe or two. You stay quiet, and don't try to run or it'll be the worse for you."

The ground was hard and cold, but Simon was tired enough to ignore it. He wished for sleep, but Daniel's questioning had brought the memory of his betrayal into sharp focus. Simon dared not sleep, in case he dreamed, in case he spoke Jessica's name.

Was this his destiny? To always betray his friends? First Elizabeth, then Matthew, and now Jessica. Perhaps even Nicholas.

Simon turned his face to the wall to hide the tears in his eyes. Behind him, Daniel sparked his tinder-box to light his pipe. Soon the stench of Daniel's tobacco drifted on the air, overwhelming the scent of the damp earth beneath Simon.

Simon recalled the day, three years ago, when Parliament's Army had caught him in the woods. They were looking for recruits, which they laughingly called volunteers. If he refused to join them, he would be considered a Royalist and killed on the spot. With a pikestaff at his neck, Simon had bartered for his freedom. He led the soldiers to where he knew a group of men worked the fields, telling the soldiers they were all fit, healthy men, far more suited to the rigors of war than was he. Simon even faked a consumptive cough to make his point.

It was after the soldiers had left him, when he hid in the trees, watching them surround the men, that Simon recognized Matthew.

He had not known that Jessica's father was in that particular field that day, but that did not assuage his guilt. Simon had exchanged his freedom for that of Matthew.

Simon had since learned that Matthew died at Naseby in 1645, but had never told Jessica of this. For the last two years she had waited in vain, not knowing that her father would never return. Simon stifled a sob. It would have been better if Elizabeth had never rescued him from Mother Chattox's wicked group. She should have left him there, to hang with the rest of them.

His self-pity was interrupted by the servant's voice.

"Lord West will see you, but he insists you are brief. I mentioned the condition of your prisoner."

Simon made to rise, but Daniel grabbed his arm again and pulled him upright.

"Let's deal with you quickly, then." Daniel pushed Simon through the door to the kitchen, where the cook waved a cloth in front of her face. The servant who had answered the door half-ran through the kitchen, then led them through corridors lined with carpet so deep it was like walking on moss. Paintings of stern gentlemen, many dressed in military clothing, frowned at Simon as he passed. He could have sworn at least one of the paintings wrinkled its nose. The servant opened a door and stood aside to let them enter. Daniel shoved Simon forward.

Pain cut into Simon's arm and through his ribs as he sprawled on the polished wooden floor of Lord West's drawing room. Lifting his head, he saw the slim, weak figure of His Lordship glaring down at him from his ornate chair. More paintings grimaced at him, delicate pottery and silver ornaments graced gleaming wooden tables near the walls. Three large, well-upholstered chairs basked in the sunlight now showing through the tall windows. Simon had never sat in a chair like that. He doubted he ever would.

"Well, Featherstone? It's early to be bringing me criminals, don't you think?" Lord West's thin, tremulous voice gave the impression of a much older man.

Simon remembered this Lord's father. Simon had drunk many a toast to this Lord's birth, because the tavern had stayed open all night in celebration. Lord West could be no more than twenty-five years old. Simon raised his head.

The man in the chair couldn't be Lord West. Simon remembered a small but healthy Lord who would often be seen in the village. It had been only four years since he had returned with Matthew Chadwick and his daughter, from one of his visits north. Since then he had seen Lord West only once, and that was shortly after his return. The Lord had since become a recluse, never seen outside his mansion.

This man bore a vague resemblance to the Lord of Simon's memory, but his clothes hung from a thin, bony body. The face staring down at him had sunken eyes and cheeks, and his lank, brown hair was streaked with gray. Did the Lord have some terrible disease? Simon tried to rise, but Daniel kicked him back to the floor.

"My apologies, My Lord. I have just arrested this man, Simon Bulcock, poaching on your land." Daniel reached down, pulled Simon's coat open and took the rabbits and hare from his belt. He lifted them for Lord West's inspection.

"I see." Lord West sniffed. "Is that smell from him or the rabbits? If it's the rabbits, they must be extraordinarily high."

"It's from him, My Lord." Daniel kicked Simon again. "He's filthy."

"Well, let's not keep him too long. Featherstone, give the rabbits to the cook. You may keep the hare as your bonus. The poacher can stand in the pillory for six hours today, and six tomorrow. He may be less offensive in the open air. You can chain him in the barn overnight. Now get the vile creature out of my house."

Daniel coughed. "There is more, my Lord. This man has information concerning the witchery that has plagued us of late."

Lord West sat up straight. "The animals?" He stared at Simon again. "Get up, you. What do you know of this?"

Simon rose to his knees, his arms clasped over his chest. "Nothing, My Lord." He yelped as Daniel cuffed his head.

"He is lying. There is a witch, draining our animals of blood and cutting them, taking just part of the carcass. Not just livestock, but foxes and badgers have been found. Sometimes deer and boar, too, their eyes and tongues cut out. He knows who is behind it."

"You are sure?" Lord West raised one eyebrow.

"Simon Bulcock never attends church, My Lord. He spends too much time with the woman Jessica Chadwick, who lives outside the village, and with another, suspected of consorting with demons."

Simon closed his eyes and wished he could do the same with his ears, but he could not shut out the conversation. The mention of tongues brought back a memory he hoped eventually to forget. Daniel had named Jessica. Did he dare name Demdike, and risk the Lord's fury?

"Who is this other?" Lord West's voice conveyed interest. Hardly surprising, since Simon knew the villagers had been complaining to his men for many months about missing or killed animals.

Daniel cleared his throat. "Well..."

"Excuse me for interrupting, My Lord. I sent this ragamuffin on an errand this morning. I see he has been intercepted." The soft voice of Nicholas Demdike drifted across the room. Simon opened his eyes to see Demdike floating along the floor, toward the Lord's chair.

"This?" Lord West indicated Simon with a wave of his hand. "Why? I have trustworthy men at my command. I could have sent one of them on this errand of yours."

"It concerns the witchcraft plaguing the village. This man brought me information late last night. Rather than disturb your Lordship, I dispatched him to summon Matthew Hopkins at first light." Demdike halted beside Lord West's chair and turned to face Simon and Daniel. "He has failed. Perhaps one of your Lordship's men would be better suited to the task after all."

Tongues. The word pressed Simon's mind, refusing to be denied. It brought the image of the iron spike in Demdike's tower into sharp clarity. Simon swallowed. It was fortunate he had not eaten that morning. Tongues. His stomach convulsed at the image.

"Nicholas? You know the identity of the witch? Why was I not informed?" Lord West whined the words, sounding like a child deprived of a treat.

"I am here to inform you now, my Lord. First though, it is most urgent that the Witchfinder is summoned."

"Yes, of course." Lord West called to the servant who waited at the door. "Find a horseman. Tell him to make all speed to find Matthew Hopkins, the Witchfinder, and tell him we have work for him here."

Daniel coughed. "Should I take this man away, my Lord?"

"What? Yes, get rid of him." Lord West turned his attention to Demdike.

Daniel half-dragged Simon from the room, back through the kitchen and out of the house. Outside, he pulled Simon upright.

"I'm not going to carry you, Bulcock. You can walk to the pillory. It's only a mile and a half."

Tongues. Simon could think of nothing else. He started walking.

"So, Bulcock, you do know who the witch is after all." Daniel increased the pressure of his grip on Simon's arm. "I'm betting it's Jessica Chadwick. Am I right?"

"No." Simon breathed the word, trying not to move his tongue. He imagined it impaled on an iron spike.

"It is, isn't it?" Daniel shoved Simon forward. Simon stumbled and fell. Daniel dragged him back to his feet.

Thoughts connected in Simon's mind. The animals, with tongues and eyes gone. Demdike watching as Simon was sentenced and dragged away. He could have said something, could at least have reduced Simon's punishment. Blood bubbling through a soldier's teeth. The iron spike. Tongues. Demdike.

"God help me." Simon saw through the illusion. Nicholas Demdike was no friend of his. Simon saw how he had been used, manipulated, fooled. Demdike wanted Jessica to take the blame for his corrupt ways, and Simon had handed her to him.

He had betrayed his last friend.

Chapter Twelve

"Where are my clothes?" Jessica stood in the hallway, which had once been her only room. There was no sign of the cabinet where she kept her clothes, indeed none of her simple furniture could be seen. "Where's my table? My bed?"

Phenex shrugged. A man approached them from the door near the front of the house. He was tall and slender, dressed in blue, and a long green snake curled around his shoulders. Phenex raised his hand.

"Andromalius. Well met, my friend. Tell me, do you know where the witch's belongings are stored?"

Andromalius stared at Jessica. "They are stored within the house."

Jessica placed her hands on her hips and tensed her jaw. "Where? What have you done with my bed, and my clothes?"

"The bed is in the bedroom. Where else would it be?" Andromalius shot a confused glance at Phenex, who stifled a chuckle.

Stomping past the tall figure, giving his snake a wide berth, Jessica headed for the stairs.

"Wait." The tone Andromalius used stopped Jessica in her tracks. She stood, refusing to turn. Foras had done the same to her. It seemed these demons could control her with a word.

"What?" She forced the word through gritted teeth.

"Listen. Sometimes those you think enemies are friends."

Jessica's shoulders relaxed. The demons were here to help. They infuriated her, controlled her to an extent, but they were not her enemies.

"I understand," she said.

"Sometimes those you think friends are enemies. Take care, young witch."

Creasing her brow, Jessica turned, intending to ask Andromalius what he meant, but he was gone. She sighed and continued upwards to the landing. Phenex followed her.

The railed landing ran along the upper floor, giving a view over the hallway below. Jessica opened doors to empty rooms until she found one containing a bed and her cabinet. She entered slowly, trying to assimilate the sight. Her bed was twice as wide as it had been, and sported four tall posts and a canopy. The mattress was thick and soft, the blankets drawn tight over it. Pillows adorned the headboard. Jessica moved to the bed and ran her hands over it, doubting its reality. Pillows!

"As I said, Malphas despises slipshod work. No doubt the rest of your furniture will receive similar attention." Phenex's voice came from behind her. She looked up to see him leaning against the doorframe. He straightened and walked toward her. "Now, Jessica, if you will dress yourself, we can speak with Foras."

Jessica crossed to her cabinet, opened it, and took out a plain green dress and cape. She started to pull her robe over her head, then noticed Phenex watching her.

"Look away, please. Let me have some privacy."

Phenex raised one eyebrow, nodded and turned his back to her. Jessica dressed quickly, always keeping an eye on the little demon.

"Ready," she said, smoothing her dress. "Let's talk to Foras."

Phenex faced her. His robe shifted and changed to become a perfect replica of her own dress. Jessica shuddered. The sight was unnerving and a little disturbing. She blew a long breath and rolled her eyes. Slipping her feet into her only pair of well-worn shoes, Jessica followed Phenex from the room. Within two strides, Phenex's feet acquired a pair of shoes to match Jessica's.

At the foot of the stairs, Jessica stopped. Her window, which had been little more than a hole in the wall with a rough frame holding four panes of low-quality glass wedged into it, now sported a smooth, white-painted frame and sill and a set of wooden shutters. It was not the frame, however, that held her attention.

Through the clear glass, the outside world shimmered, darkened and finally vanished. Jessica ran to the window. Sunlight brightened the windowsill and cast a shadow of the frame on the floor, yet through the window she saw nothing.

"Phenex, something is wrong." Jessica leaned close to the glass. She felt the warmth of the sun but still she saw nothing.

"That's the Hiding." Phenex stood beside her, his hands on the windowsill. "The beginning of it, anyway. Seere and Bifrons are creating it now. When it is complete, you will see through your windows again."

"What is it? How does it work?"

"No time for explanations now. Come, Foras will be waiting."

Phenex took Jessica's hand and led her from the window. She gazed at the darkness, wondering if any human could ever become powerful enough to perform such magic. She allowed Phenex to lead her through the kitchen, where her table now stood, smooth and polished. As they approached the door at the rear of the kitchen, it swung open.

"There you are, Phenex. Foras wants your help." A guttural voice issued from a toothed owl-beak set in a feathered face. Two huge, round, gloss-black eyes stared at Jessica from above the beak. Jessica screamed and tried to run, but Phenex kept his grip on her hand.

She struggled to escape, but Phenex's tiny hand might as well have been made of stone. The creature entered the kitchen. The thing had the torso and forelegs of a dog, but the hind part of its body tapered into a thick serpent's tail. It moved toward her, its forelegs walking while its tail writhed and pushed. Jessica fell to the floor, still trying to escape Phenex's grip. Phenex turned his smile to her.

"Peace, Jessica. It is only Amon. He will not harm you."

The creature called Amon halted, backing off a little. "Does my appearance alarm you? Those of us who rarely visit humanity have not mastered the art of imitating your shape. Some of us are stuck with the distorted bodies we were given when we fell."

Jessica stared into the golden eyes of Phenex and waited until the pounding of her heart slowed. She looked again at Amon, using her senses to try to probe the soul within his twisted form. His power excluded her, although she could see concern reflected in his huge eyes. Rising to her feet, Jessica shook herself.

"I am pleased to make your acquaintance, Lord Amon." She wondered if she should curtsey, or hold out her hand, but the repulsive sight of Amon held her back.

"My title is Marquis, but you may call me Amon." His beak chattered as he laughed.

"I am Jessica Chadwick."

"Oh, we all know who you are. You are the one who will bring the Golab to our trap."

A chill seeped into Jessica's bones. These demons saw her as bait, nothing more. As though he read her thoughts, Amon continued.

"We will see you are not harmed. You are important to us." With a nod to Phenex, Amon moved toward the door to the hallway, calling back to her as he left. "You must go into the circle, while it is still safe. Foras is expecting you."

"This way." Phenex led Jessica to the open door, through which the smell of early-morning grass flowed. Jessica stepped through the door and gasped.

Two straight gravel paths diverged at her feet, heading into the distance. Where there should have been trees, scattered on uneven ground, there was over half a mile of flat lawn. Surrounding this, glittering in the sunlight streaming over the house, stood the circle of tall windows on the inside of the circular corridor she had glimpsed earlier. Patches of trimmed shrubbery dotted the lawn, and in its centre stood a tall stone block. Two figures moved near the block. One was unmistakably Foras, the other strutted as though walking on tiptoe.

"Malphas did this also?" Jessica followed Phenex across the lawn, walking between the paths. The damp grass soaked her feet through the holes in her shoes.

"No, this is Foras's work. Malphas builds. Foras plants." Phenex increased his pace. Jessica struggled to keep up.

"My garden. My herbs. What has he done with them?"

"They will be replanted somewhere else. Foras will not harm anything that grows in the ground."

Jessica took a deep breath of the clear air. Unlike the usual forest scent, this garden filled her senses with spring flowers and trimmed grass. They passed one of the shrubberies, and Jessica stopped to examine a bush. She ran her fingers over its leaves, enjoying the aroma it released.

"Rosemary." Jessica marveled at Foras's skill. It should take this bush many years to reach such a size.

"Foras is waiting." There was a hint of sadness in Phenex's voice. "The trap is almost complete. I fear your enjoyment of this garden will be brief." He pulled at Jessica's hand.

Foras and his companion turned to face them as they approached. The demon with Foras had an elongated head, and as they drew closer Jessica recognized it as that of a horse. It must be the demon Foras called just as she fell asleep last night. She struggled to recall its name.

"Orobas." Phenex smiled up at her. "That is the name you are searching for."

"You can see my thoughts?"

"Magic flows through you, Jessica, and you have learned neither to control nor hide it. You are in a state of change, your power is wide open, and it is a time of great risk for you." The smile left

Phenex's lips. "You have yet to choose your path. The dark magics will tempt you, and they are difficult to resist."

"I will resist." Jessica recalled tales of the corrupt and terrible methods used by her great-aunt. Fingers and skulls from corpses were their most powerful talismans. Magic of that sort held no appeal for Jessica.

"I am glad to hear it." Foras said, as Jessica and Phenex reached the stone block in the centre of the garden. "If you were to turn against us, all this work would be in vain."

"Foras—" Jessica began, but Foras had already turned to Phenex.

"We have need of your artistic talents, Phenex." He handed Goetia to the child-demon. "Inscribe our sigils around the circle, behind the glass. Mine should be placed outside the circle, on the south side of the house. It will warn me if trouble should arise, and allow me to come and go at will."

Phenex accepted the book. "If the Golab should escape, you will not be able to contain it alone."

"I can use your sigils to call the rest of you, should the need arise."

"Foras—" Jessica tried again. This time Phenex interrupted.

"What of this block?" He indicated the stone behind Foras. A granite cube, ten feet to a side, oppressed the otherwise beautiful garden with its somber minimalism. "It is an uninspiring monument."

"The block supports the upper bowl of the trap." Foras regarded it for a moment. "You can make a statue of it, if you wish."

"Foras—" Jessica's patience snapped. She grabbed Goetia from Phenex. The three demons turned to face her.

"What is this?" Foras moved to retrieve the book, but Jessica backed away.

"You say I am important to you, but you ignore me as though I were a child. You have done all this to my house, my garden, without consulting me. Does my opinion count for nothing?"

Orobas moved toward Jessica. "You are important. Without you, we have no hope of capturing the creature." He lowered his long white head so that his dark-brown eyes met hers. "In the matter of this construction, you must trust us."

"There is no time for such petulance." Foras moved beside Orobas. Green light burned in his eyes. "Give me the book."

"No." Jessica opened Goetia and grasped one of its pages between thumb and forefinger. "Listen to me, or I will tear the pages from this book."

"Are you a fool?" Foras grew in stature, as he had when Jessica first called him, but this time his skin took on the gnarled appearance of an ancient oak and his arms stretched above Jessica. "Do you not realize who you address? We can kill you with a thought, strip the flesh from your bones with a word, and send your soul into torment with a gesture."

"No." Jessica fought the tremor in her voice. "You can do none of these things to me. Murderers do not go to Heaven."

Orobas stood between Foras and Jessica. "You cannot harm her, Foras. I will not permit it."

Phenex moved to Jessica's side. "Foras, you must control yourself. This action will not help our cause."

Above them, Foras's elongated fingers twitched. His face, which had grown a surround of oak leaves, lost its fury. Foras resumed human form and bowed his head.

"Forgive me, Jessica. We have waited a long time for an opportunity such as this." He looked up. "Now, the book, if you please."

"Hear my opinion first." Jessica closed Goetia and held it to her chest.

"I will hear you, while Phenex inscribes the sigils." Foras reached for Goetia.

Blue light flared around his hand. Foras drew back. A frown creased his face as he inspected his fingers.

"It seems this witch is not one to be trifled with, Foras." Phenex spoke through laughter.

"Indeed. She has little need of protection." Orobas joined Phenex's mirth.

"Very well." Foras sighed. "Speak, but be brief."

"I—" Jessica faltered. The blue flare that had repulsed Foras came from her, but it was no spell she knew. "Did I hurt you?"

"No, you did not." Foras held up his hand. "If your power were more focused, perhaps you would have caused pain." He raised one eyebrow. "The flare would have killed a human. Do you understand how you formed it?"

Jessica shook her head.

"Then you must keep your temper in check, until you have control over your magic. Now, what is it you wanted to say?"

Jessica swallowed. "The sigils. Phenex should carve them all. Sixty-nine in the circle. Yours, Foras, south of the house. Malphas should have his sigil within the house. It's part of the circle, and he built it."

"Ridiculous." Foras laughed. "Sixty of these sigils represent those who follow Lucifer and Moloch. They will not help us."

"No, but their power will be drawn here, to strengthen the trap. Besides, in three hundred years your number might increase. What if one of the dark ones joins your cause, but his sigil is not here?" Jessica said.

"She has a point, Foras." Orobas rubbed his chin. "I know Buer, for one, has doubts about his allegiance with Hell."

"I agree with Jessica." Phenex said. "But your number adds up to only seventy-one, Jessica. Who have you missed?"

"Asmodeus." Jessica spoke into Foras's eyes. "The owner of the Golab. He must be represented here. I suggest his sigil should be in the centre, with a statue of him carved from that stone block."

Foras stared at her, then at the block, then at Phenex. "What say you, Phenex? Can you form an image of Asmodeus here?"

"With ease, Foras." Phenex walked to the block. "This is good stone. I can cut the detail easily."

"Then it shall be as our witch decrees." Foras lifted Goetia from Jessica's unresisting hands and passed it to Phenex. He looked over his shoulder at Jessica. "I hope our discussions will not always be so—violent."

Jessica stretched her shoulders. "That depends on whether you listen to me." The blue flare had given her confidence, though she had no idea how she had produced it. Somewhere within herself, Jessica held magic of sufficient strength to repel a President of Hell. Perhaps she was not as helpless as she had supposed.

Phenex winked at her, then ran across the lawn toward a door set in the long, circular corridor. Orobas stood beside her. Foras folded his arms and stared at her.

"You are full of impertinence, for a neophyte. However, you are right. Without you, we have no chance of success. I will recognize your importance." He raised his hand, one finger extended. "But not your authority. You are inexperienced, so when the time comes, you must do as you are told. We know this Golab, you do not. Your dissent may slow us and allow it to escape. Do you agree?"

"I agree, Foras." Jessica nodded. "I have another question."

Foras closed his eyes for a moment. "You surprise me." The curl in his lip made his sarcasm clear.

"Amon said I should enter the circle while it is safe. Phenex said my enjoyment of this garden would be brief. Why? What did they mean?"

"The size of the circle has a reason, and that reason lies in the range of the Golab's influence. The Golab takes its power from women, so once it is trapped here, no woman must enter. Inside the circle, the Golab can call to them, entice them, and draw them toward itself. Outside the circle, it cannot reach them. So you must never enter this garden once the Golab is trapped. If it draws enough power, it might be able to free itself."

"You mean women must be excluded from here for three hundred years?" Jessica stared around herself at the perfect lawns, the shrubberies, the spring flowers opening. "How?"

"The Hiding will protect this from prying eyes." Orobas said. "The garden can be entered only from the house."

"Surely someone will live in this house after me? How will you keep women out?" Jessica looked from one demon to the other. "You haven't thought of it, have you?"

"We are not perfect." Foras avoided her gaze. "If we were, we would not be the Fallen." He looked at Jessica. "You raise a valid point. However, we have time to consider this after the Golab is trapped. If we fail in that, nothing else matters."

"That's another question. You have not said how I should bring the Golab here." Jessica narrowed her eyes. "Have you thought of that?"

"We have." Foras returned her gaze. "You are to go into the village today and arouse the suspicions of the people there. They will send the Witchfinder to test you. When he arrives, run inside, through the tunnel and into the trap. He will follow."

"What if he catches me before I reach your trap?"

"We will delay him." Orobas placed his strong, hard hand on her shoulder.

"I don't know." Jessica shook her head. "Although I had planned to visit the fair today. I wanted to sell some herbs. Where are my herbs, Foras?"

"On the north side of the house. They are more potent than before." Foras smiled. "Go to the village, sell your herbs. Perform some small magics, just enough to make them suspect you. Trust us, you will not be alone."

"You cannot visit the village." Jessica took a step back. "None of you. They will burn me immediately if I am seen with demons."

"Not if you are seen with a horse, surely?" Orobas dropped to all fours. His body grew, his hands became hooves. Jessica stared into the brown eyes of a perfectly ordinary-looking white stallion.

"We are adept at not being seen." Foras grinned. "Go with

Orobas. I will send Bifrons and Seere when the Hiding is completed, to ensure your safety." He lifted Jessica onto Orobas's back. "I will speak to you when you return."

"I don't know how to ride a horse." Jessica leaned forward, her arms around Orobas's neck.

"Not too tight, please. I will not move too fast." Orobas turned his head to wink at her, then set off at a canter toward the house.

Above the house, and around the circle, the sky melted into a haze that rose rapidly, like a curtain lifting over a clear dome.

Chapter Thirteen

The bright ribbons of the maypole fluttered in the breeze. The little village square filled with people as the morning progressed, some pausing to stare at Simon but most ignoring him. Nothing had been thrown at him yet, but it was early. Everyone was busy, preparing their Mayday celebrations.

Simon twisted his hands in yet another attempt to alleviate the discomfort in his wrists. Nothing worked. The rope Daniel had tied them with chafed his skin. Simon let his head hang in the wooden pillory, wishing his wrists had fit the holes. If they had, Daniel would not have tied them to stop him slipping them out.

The coarse wood of the pillory hurt his throat but Simon ignored it. He knew there would be worse to come when the Mayday frenzy took hold of the village. They would throw things then, vegetables, excrement, dead rats. Maybe even stones. A well-placed stone could end his misery, release him from his guilt.

"Hey, Simon. So you've been caught at last."

Simon looked up, then glanced left and right. Daniel had left him, but the voice was not Daniel's anyway. It was a voice he knew, although his exhausted mind could put no name or face to it.

"Simon, you old bugger. Are you sleeping up there?" The speaker appeared at his left, staggering a little as he rounded the stage that held the pillory. Robert Davies, the town's joiner, wheelwright, cooper and undertaker. It would have been Robert who put up the maypole, though now it seemed he may need its support himself. Robert's father had constructed the pillory in which Simon now stood.

Simon tried to speak, but managed only a dry cough. Robert lurched forward and climbed up to face Simon. He held on to the pillory and lifted his tankard to Simon's lips.

"Here, have a swallow of good ale. Twenty barrels came in from Marchway this morning. It's going to be a good Mayday."

After quenching his thirst on Robert's generosity, Simon found his voice.

"Are there any barrels left? You look as though you've drunk a few of them already."

Robert roared with laughter, swinging away from Simon as he held the pillory.

"Some, Simon. I'll keep a few quarts back for you. Will you be long?"

"Two days."

"Two?" Robert's face assumed an almost-sober expression. "What did you do?"

"I poached a hare and some rabbits." He had also betrayed Jessica, but that would merit more than the pillory. His punishment for that crime came from within himself.

"Two days for a few fur balls. That's unfair." Robert let go of the pillory and dropped to the ground, stumbling a little but holding his beer upright. "You've been good to most folk here, Simon. We've all eaten a little of your spoils."

He lifted his tankard. "I'll put word around, and see you're not pelted today. You won't have to worry about tomorrow; we'll all be too hung over to throw anything." Robert took a deep swallow, and then headed toward a group near the maypole, calling out names as he walked.

Simon hung his head again. He didn't deserve this kindness. Yes, he had shared his stolen meat with those in the town who were hungry, with those who couldn't pay, as well as with those who could.

He had betrayed Jessica, the last of her family, that harmless, helpful girl who had shown nothing but kindness to all who met her. He knew she was a witch, but she had caused no harm. No, the mutilated animals were nothing to do with her. Simon now knew who was responsible for that.

Demdike. The thought of that name made Simon's lips draw back over his teeth. All this time he had trusted Nicholas Demdike, believed his promises to teach him magic and to look after Jessica.

He should have known, should have seen through Demdike's bewitchments. Elizabeth had known. When Nicholas Demdike tried to join her group, she had sent him away in fury. She had warned Simon, but Demdike's subtle enchantments had seduced him. When Simon fled here with Matthew and Jessica after Elizabeth's execution, Simon had been surprised to find Demdike back in his old tower.

Simon closed his eyes. The tower had been Demdike's home for as long as he could remember. Why, then, did his mind now shout doubts into his head? The tower had always been there, but his mind insisted on showing him a blank space beside Lord

West's mansion. Simon concentrated, trying to sort real memories from illusion.

Something thudded against the pillory beside his head. Simon opened his eyes in time to see a clod of earth flying at his face. He tried to avoid it, but the pillory allowed no movement. The soil hit his cheek and shattered, showering dirt over his face. Simon grunted in pain.

Someone cheered. Simon blinked dirt from his eyes. Two soldiers, in the red jackets and steel plate uniform of the Roundhead army, grinned and slapped each other on the back. Four pikestaffs lay on the ground behind them, each one sixteen feet long and tipped with a sharp steel point.

"Fine shot, George. Let's see if I can do better." One of the men bent to the ground and lifted a stone the size of his fist. "This one for his eye." He took aim.

Simon squinted at the stone. The men stood some ten feet away, so if the stone struck his head it might kill him. The soldier closed one eye to line up his shot. Simon wondered if his death would be quick or lingering. Quick would be better. Lingering was what he could expect from Demdike. The soldier drew back his arm.

"Hoi! What are you two doing?" Two more soldiers appeared at the door of the tavern. The speaker sounded as though he had some kind of authority even though his armor looked no different from that worn by the other three. He strode toward the pair in front of Simon, followed by the fourth soldier.

"Just time for a quick throw." The stone flew from the soldier's hand and struck Simon on the right side of his mouth. The impact threw Simon's head to his left. Bright lights exploded in his eyes. Simon struggled to breathe as warm fluid filled his mouth. He spat the liquid out and hung his head. Through tear-blurred eyes, he watched red streams fall from his mouth to pool on the ground. Probing the tender wound with his tongue, he discovered at least two of his teeth were gone.

"Stop that. We are not here for you to amuse yourselves." The leader of the group moved forward to inspect Simon's wound. "It was a good shot, though. Maybe we should take your pikestaff away and give you a bag of stones."

The soldiers laughed. Simon blinked until he could see the man facing him. He looked to be around thirty, muscular and well fed. Brown hair showed under his blackened steel helmet and a long scar ran across his left cheek, ending close to one of his deep brown eyes. The soldier stood with one hand on the hilt of his sword and breathed the scent of Marchway ale into Simon's face.

"Looks like you'll have a scar to rival my own." The soldier ran his finger across his own scar. "Although mine came to me in battle. Yours is the mark of a coward and a criminal." He turned away and walked toward his men. "Don't worry about your face, criminal. It wasn't a pretty one anyway." The men joined him in laughter. The one named George picked up a stone.

"Shall we pelt him a little more?"

"No." Their leader took the stone from George's hand and dropped it to the ground. "We have work to do, and we're not getting very far. Nobody at the tavern knew anything, although most of them are already so drunk they wouldn't notice if our whole army came through here."

"What about him?" One of the men indicated Simon. "He's probably the only sober man in the whole place."

"Him?" The leader faced Simon. "What can a common criminal tell us?" He blew a long breath. "Well, I suppose it's worth a try."

He climbed onto the wooden stage and leaned on the pillory, then grabbed Simon's hair and pulled his head up.

"What do you say, criminal? Will you answer my questions, or should I let my men have a little more target practice?"

"I'll answer." Simon mumbled through his shattered mouth. Several villagers gathered to watch, including Robert, who shook his head sadly. Simon knew they dared not interfere with these men. That could result in the village being ransacked by the whole regiment.

"Good. Now, we are looking for three deserters from our army. They will be dressed as we are, and we know they came in this direction." The soldier tightened his grip on Simon's hair. "Have you seen them?"

"Yes." Simon gasped the word. "I know where they are." He also knew their fate, but considered this an unwise time to mention it.

"Really?" The grip on Simon's hair relaxed. "Where?"

"They are in Demdike's tower, beside Lord West's home." Simon's mind raced. If four soldiers arrived in daylight, with witnesses, Demdike might not find them so easy to kill. When they found their men, they must surely attack Demdike for what he had done to them.

"Who is this Demdike, and why is he sheltering deserters? Is he a Royalist?"

"He is a witch. He captured your men." Simon's jaw ached with the effort of speech.

"I see." The soldier released Simon's hair, letting his head fall. Simon's throat hit the lower edge of the pillory's hole hard enough to make him retch. The soldier jumped from the stage and spoke to his men, then with some of the villagers. The four soldiers picked up their pikes and headed in the direction of Lord West's mansion.

Simon tried to call out, to warn them to beware of Demdike's enchantments, but the pain in his mouth and throat prevented him. All he managed to produce was a strangled gasp.

"I thought you were done for." Robert's voice came to Simon through a haze of pain. "Why did you send them to Lord West?"

"He'd have sent them anywhere to make them stop." A woman's voice came from the crowd.

Simon couldn't make out who it was.

"Can't blame him," said another. Murmurs of assent ran through the crowd, which gradually dispersed.

Soon only Robert stood facing Simon.

"I sent them to Demdike." Simon managed to mutter through his pain. Robert whistled.

"He won't thank you for that." Robert looked into the remains of his beer. "Maybe they'll kill him and do us all a favor." He glanced up at Simon. "If they don't, you'd best get as far away as possible, as soon as you're out of that thing."

Simon's body shook, caught between laughter and tears. Choking, wheezing sounds escaped his throat. Through it all he registered Robert backing away, toward the tavern. Simon wanted to call out, wanted to shout what he knew to the whole village, but his rapidly-swelling injuries erupted in agony when he tried to speak above a whisper.

He had so much to say, but he had been deprived of the means to say it. Running from Demdike was no use. There was nowhere he could hide. If the soldiers failed, then Simon would die at Demdike's hands, and he had no need to imagine the manner of his death.

Simon let his head hang. Tears, dirt and blood fell from his face to the wooden stage. Whether Demdike lived or died, there was nobody to protect Jessica. Simon once more cursed the day Elizabeth had saved him from the gallows.

Chapter Fourteen

Jessica stood with Orobas in the hallway of her expanding house, facing the north wall. She clung to her wicker basket and wondered if she had enough power to blast a hole in the wall.

Orobas, once more in near-human form, shuffled his feet. "I'm sure Malphas won't be long."

Jessica sniffed, not trusting herself to comment. Where her herbs were supposed to be, the circular corridor to the rear of the house and the Hiding to the front blocked the way. Jessica considered trying to call up her blue flare, but she had no idea how powerful it could be. It might punch a neat hole in the wall, or it might destroy the house.

"Ah, here he is," Orobas said.

Malphas appeared from the door in the south wall, the one Jessica had not yet investigated. He half-walked, half-hopped to where Jessica stood, tapping her foot.

"Amon said you found a flaw in my design. Where is it?"

"Here." Jessica waved her hand at the wall. Malphas moved forward to inspect it. "I see nothing."

"Precisely. There's no door."

"Door?" Malphas turned his head to aim one eye at Jessica. "Door to where?"

"To my garden." Jessica raised her hand to forestall Malphas's obvious retort. "Not the circle. My own garden."

"Ah." Malphas's beak bobbed in understanding. "Yes, of course. This has been a rather hurried construction. One or two small details must have escaped me." He drew a rectangle on the wall with the point of his trowel, then muttered a few words in his guttural croak. The wall within the rectangle dissolved into dust, which faded into nothing before it could settle.

"Thank you." Jessica stepped through the opening, followed by Orobas. Behind her, Malphas was already fitting a lintel and painted wooden frame into the hole.

The blank inner wall of the circle curved away to Jessica's right, while on the left she saw the road and the woods. The view was clear, though it shimmered when she moved her eyes. She frowned at Orobas.

"When we went outside, all we saw were woods beside the house. From this side, there's my garden but there seems to be nothing between us and the road."

"The Hiding is complete." Orobas bared his teeth in a grin. "You should not attempt to pass through from this side. It will be uncomfortable. I will demonstrate what happens from the other side later, when we leave."

Jessica pursed her lips. She wanted to appear calm and in control, but she ached to know how the Hiding worked. First, though, she needed herbs to sell at the fair. Jessica turned her attention to her plants for the first time since entering the garden and groaned aloud. She should have expected this.

Showing a total disregard for season, Foras had coaxed all of her herbs into full growth. There was basil, looking as though it was about to flower. Coriander and parsley overflowed their beds. Tarragon, which should be just sprouting, had already reached three feet in height. Belson emerged from the tarragon and mewed at her, then sat on the path and licked his paws.

Jessica blew a long breath. If Foras wanted her to raise suspicions of witchcraft, all she had to do was turn up at the village with an abundance of fresh herbs. She placed her basket on the ground and took out her knife and twine. Jessica cut bundles of each herb and tied them with twine. The bundles she laid on the path behind her. When she had finished, she walked back along the path, waving her hands and murmuring one of her mother's spells over each of the bundles.

Vapor rose from each bundle as the herbs dried. Satisfied, Jessica collected the bundles and placed them in her basket, with the knife and twine at the bottom. She returned to Orobas, waiting at the door, who regarded her with his head on one side.

"Why?" he said. "Surely the plants are better used fresh?"

"I'm not going to make it too easy." Jessica swept past him and opened the new door to her house. Belson brushed past her legs.

"Too many fresh herbs on the first of May will raise more suspicion than I'd like." Jessica crossed the hallway to her front door. Orobas followed her through the house.

Outside, Jessica scanned the road. "You'd better turn into a horse again, Orobas."

"I already have, Jessica."

"Good." Jessica turned to face Orobas and moved her basket away from his enquiring nose. "Just remember, when we get there, that horses don't speak."

"They speak to me." Orobas lifted his head.

"Well, they don't speak to people." A smile twitched Jessica's mouth, despite her attempt to appear stern. What was Foras thinking, letting her visit the village with a talking horse? "People are going to wonder how I acquired a horse anyway, much less one that can talk. Now, show me this Hiding and then we can be on our way."

"Certainly." Orobas moved to the side of the house. "Here it is."

Jessica stood at his side. "All I see are trees."

"Exactly. We have used this before. Did you ever hear of a place called Eden?"

"Eden is real?" Jessica stepped forward and put out her hand. From her garden, the Hiding appeared to run from the front wall of her house, but no matter how far she reached past the wall, she felt nothing.

"We are real. Why would you doubt Eden?" Orobas winked at her, then put his head behind her and nudged her forward. "Walk beside the house."

Jessica walked onto the grassy bank, among the trees, until she had passed the rear of the house.

"I felt nothing." She turned to Orobas, but he had vanished. So had the road, and her house. Jessica stared around herself. The place looked familiar, she knew she had been here before, but her mind struggled to reconcile what she saw with what she knew.

"Impressive, is it not?" Orobas appeared beside her.

"What happened? I felt no magic. I recognize this place, but if I am right then we cannot be here. It is more than half a mile from my house."

"Indeed it is. We are at the other end of the Hiding." Orobas's brown eyes twinkled. "A trick of Seere's. He can fold space and time."

"Fold—" Jessica shook her head.

"Put simply, when we entered the Hiding at your house, we immediately passed to the far side of the garden. There is another spell involved which removes doubt from the mind, so nobody will realize that the space between ever existed. It won't work on you because you've seen the garden." Orobas stared at her. "It is a difficult concept. Seere can explain, though I doubt his explanation will be of much help. Now, shall we go back to the house, and begin our journey?"

"No." Jessica squinted at the trees, but could detect no magical screen. "No, we are closer to the village here. This way." She led Orobas away from the Hiding, occasionally stealing a glance backwards. "The village is only a little further."

They walked among the trees, along paths already bordered by lengthening grasses and the first shoots of bluebells. Jessica breathed deeply of the forest air, savoring the spring scents of renewed growth. This was the domain of Foras, the domain of growing things, of green shoots and bright flowers. The dried herbs in Jessica's basket seemed an anathema here, a basket of dead things in a world of new life.

"Orobas." Jessica spoke softly. "What is Foras like?"

"Like?" Orobas mulled the question. "What are his desires, you mean?"

"No, I mean what is he like as a man? As a demon."

"He is as you see him. We all are. We do not practice the deceptions of our darker brethren."

"That's not what I meant." Jessica kept her attention on the ground. "Is he—do you all have wives?"

"Oh, I see." Orobas snickered. "You are ignorant of our state. We have fallen from grace for different reasons. Some of us had wives once. Some fell with Semjaza, when he led the way to consort with the daughters of men."

Heat warmed Jessica's face. "Foras was one of these?"

"He was, as was Bifrons, Seere, and Andromalius. Among others. Their children were stronger, larger, faster, and more intelligent than were human children. Nephilim. I believe they are mentioned in your holy book."

"So their wives are all long dead." Jessica kept her head down to hide her growing smirk.

"Long ago, yes. The Nephilim were left uncontrolled and caused considerable havoc. They came to realize that they were not as other men and they took advantage of their power and strength. Many died at their hands. As a result, all those who consorted with human women were punished." Orobas paused. "They will not make that mistake again."

"Oh." Jessica missed her footing and stumbled on the rough ground.

"You must ignore what your heart tells you, Jessica. Foras cannot consort with a human woman. It will set back all he has done to gain redemption."

"I understand, Orobas." Jessica sighed. The sounds of merrymaking drifted through the trees. "The village is close. You have to keep silent now."

They emerged from the trees onto the road leading into the village. From here, the cheers and whoops of the fair were clear. The music of fiddle and drum drifted through the air. Jessica took a deep breath and led Orobas into the narrow street that led them into the village square.

Yesterday she would have gazed in envy at the expertly built houses, both old and new, with their multiple rooms and upper floors. Today she allowed herself a smug smile. Compared to her house, these were now hovels. Their timber-made upper floors overhung the brick-built ground floor, paint peeled from the woodwork, and gaps showed in the cement between some of the bricks.

"Malphas would be furious," Jessica muttered.

"Indeed he would," Orobas replied, then nodded his head at Jessica's hard stare.

"Jessica. Good to see you." The lopsided grin of Tom Barnett, the weaver, shone at them from his doorway. "I was just on my way to join the fun."

"Oh, I don't have time for fun, Tom. I'm here to sell my herbs." Jessica held her basket up for Tom's inspection.

"A good batch this year." Tom raised an eyebrow. "And I see you have a horse. Why are you not riding it? Is it for sale?"

"The herbs are last year's, dried, and no, my horse is not for sale. He's—" Jessica faltered. What reason could she give for walking a horse into the village, if not to sell it?

Fortunately, Tom appeared not to notice her hesitation. He walked around Orobas, then pulled the horse's mouth open and inspected the teeth within.

"A fine animal. Should get you a good price. I've no use for one myself, but Dan Featherstone could do with something to ride on. He's too old and too fat for a bailiff." Tom sniffed. "Careful though, he'll haggle hard."

"He's not for sale." Jessica repeated. "These herbs are all I'm selling today. Can I interest you in some? A little tarragon, to liven up your chicken dinner? Coriander and parsley, for soups and stuffings? I have some wintergreen that's a good cure for a headache."

Tom shook his head. "I know little about cooking. Although here comes Miriam. She might be interested."

Miriam, Tom's wife, barreled along the street toward them. Her blue skirts swished around her feet, her arms, elbows bent and fists clenched, swung at her sides. Jessica glanced at Tom, but he was still looking Orobas over. Miriam's face bore the expression of someone about to give vent to a long-hidden fury.

"Thomas Barnett! You get away from there." Miriam's strident voice filled the street. A few people turned their heads to look, but most of the village was by now in the square.

"What?" Tom looked around. "What are you going on about, Miriam? It's only Jessica, selling her herbs."

"Well, I've been hearing things about this herb-seller." Miriam stopped a few feet from Jessica, her eyes blazing. "You come away, Thomas." She grabbed Tom's arm and dragged him back toward the square.

"Goodbye then, Jessica." Tom called back. "Good luck with your herbs, and your horse." He turned to his wife and said something, but by now, they were too far away for Jessica to hear their conversation.

"What was all that about? Why did your friend want to see my teeth?" Orobas whispered in her ear.

"Quiet! He thought you were for sale." Jessica stared along the street. At the far end, a group of women chatted. Their frequent glances in her direction made Jessica uneasy.

"You'd better go back into the woods, Orobas. Something has made these people more suspicious of me than usual. It's best if I'm not seen with something as valuable as a horse."

"I have to watch over you. That's why I'm here." Orobas tilted his head.

"Yes, but you'll do more harm than good. Look, Foras said you could do nothing to interfere in human lives. So, even if I get into trouble, you can't help me in the middle of the village. If the mood of these people looks nasty, I'll run to the woods."

Orobas's long mane shook. "Your purpose here was to arouse suspicion. If those suspicions already exist, that purpose is achieved. We can leave."

"You don't understand human life, Orobas. I have to eat. If I want bread, I have to buy flour. To do that I need money. To get money I have to sell my herbs."

Orobas stamped his hoof. "I will wait here. You are right, I cannot interfere with humans, but from here, I can watch you. Stay in sight. If the need arises, I will help if I can."

He lowered his head. "If I cannot, I will fetch Bifrons and Seere. Seere looks somewhat like one of you. Bifrons—" He looked away. "Bifrons does not, but he is less concerned with the morality of interference." Orobas blew a breath. "If the truth be told, Bifrons struggles with morality of any kind."

Jessica puffed out her cheeks. Orobas was clearly not going to move. "Very well. I will stay on this corner of the square, where you can see me. Now, I really have to sell some of these herbs."

She turned away and started along the street. The group of women had stopped their conversation and now stared openly at her. Jessica avoided eye contact, aware that they had seen her talking to a horse. They were too far away to hear what she and Orobas said, but her behavior would certainly seem odd to them. These women would have been potential customers but Jessica decided to move on.

The people of the village had congregated in the main square. Beneath their feet, the grass had been trampled into mud in many places. Young men and women danced around the maypole, weaving the ribbons into a criss-cross pattern as they drew ever closer to the pole. Children gathered around the baker's stall, where hot buns and a variety of sweets were displayed. Their warm, fresh-baked smell filled the air.

A fiddler and a drummer played a fast jig in the far corner, between the maypole and the tavern. On the platform in the centre of the square, his back to Jessica, a man stood in the pillory. He was only some forty or so feet away, but Jessica could not make out whom the bedraggled prisoner might be.

He sagged, his knees bent, and would clearly collapse if he were not supported by the pillory. Jessica averted her eyes from the sight. Whoever he was, he was in no state to be standing there. She wondered what crime he committed to be punished so cruelly.

Jessica approached a woman near the baker's stall. She held up her basket to display her bundles of herbs.

"Dried herbs, farthing a bundle?"

The woman narrowed her eyes and curled her lip, then stalked away into the crowd. Jessica approached another, and another, all with the same result. Puzzled, she examined the herbs in her basket. They seemed perfectly all right to her.

Jessica leaned against the wall of the butcher's shop and watched the people moving around the fair. She had never encountered such rudeness here before, and it confused her. She was about to try another potential customer when Tom appeared in the butcher's doorway.

"Hello again, Tom."

Tom met her gaze, then turned his face away. He walked past

Jessica's Trap

Jessica and stopped beside her, on the opposite side to the butcher's door.

"You should go home, Jessica. There are stories going around. The women are gossiping about you."

"What's this?" Jessica sucked at her lip. She had performed no magic here as yet. Did they already think she was a witch? Or perhaps...

"Tom, I've noticed the women won't speak to me. Most of the men won't even look at me. Does your wife think that you and I—"

"No, no, good gracious no, nothing like that." Tom's face flushed. "No, if that were all, it would not be so bad." He produced a silver sixpence from his pocket. "Here, take this. It's more than you'll make today. Just get out of here while you can." He placed the coin in her hand.

Jessica stared at the shining sixpence. "Tom, this will buy most of my basket." She held the coin out to him. "I can't accept this."

"Take it, please, and get away." Tom stood a little way off now, facing away from Jessica as though ignoring her. "The gossips are calling you a witch. You know what that can mean these days."

Jessica drew a sharp breath. So, the village suspected her of witchcraft anyway. Orobas was right. They could leave. She started back toward the street where Orobas waited, but paused as she passed Tom. Jessica rearranged the herbs in her basket while she spoke in a low voice.

"Thank you, Tom. I have one thing to ask. Do you know if the Witchfinder is coming?"

Tom shivered. "Don't even mention him. I don't believe all this witchcraft nonsense, but the atrocities that terrible man and his friends have carried out are all too real. I hope this is all just Mayday gossip, which will be forgotten tomorrow. If not, I will find a way to warn you."

Jessica nodded. It would indeed be useful to know when the Witchfinder was on his way. "You can get a message to me by way of Simon Bulcock. He visits me sometimes."

"Not today I can't, and not tomorrow." Tom nodded at the pillory. "He has two days to stand there, so I'm told."

Jessica's vision blurred. The sounds of the fair became dull and distant. The fiddle, now shrill, sounded like a cat wailing in the night, while the drum's fast beat mirrored the pounding of her pulse. Her basket fell from her hand.

"You didn't know?" Tom placed his hand on her arm. "I'm sorry."

Jessica shrugged his hand away and started toward the pillory. If Foras wanted her to use magic here, then she would do just that. Control or no, she was going to use that flare of hers to blast the pillory into matchwood. Jessica barged past anyone who stood in her way. Their protests and mutterings went unheard.

She arrived at the platform and looked up at Simon's limp body. From behind, he looked dead. He certainly smelled dead. Slowly, she made her way around the pillory. At the front, its base bore a splatter of drying blood. Jessica composed herself, prepared to face the worst, and turned her face upwards to Simon's.

"There's the witch!" The shout came from behind her. Jessica stared at the shattered remains of Simon's mouth, at the dirt and blood-caked bruises that covered his cheeks and throat, and let her rage build.

Chapter Fifteen

Simon tried to swallow but the effort tore at his throat. He pushed his tongue between his cracked lips and tried to moisten them. His tongue, though, was as dry and as swollen as his lips.

Some of the villagers had tried to give him water, a little while ago. When they found he could not drink, they had pressed a wet cloth to his lips. It had helped, at first, but the moisture had since dried. How long had he stood here? The passage of time meant nothing now. Every moment was an eternity of pain.

The pillory chafed Simon's wrists and neck, but he had no strength left to support his own weight. Children's shrieks, the wail of the fiddle, drunken cheers, and the drumbeat, all drove like nails of iron into his skull. He had lost all sensation in his hands.

He forced his eyes to focus on the tavern door. Daniel had gone in there with some of Lord West's men, hours—or perhaps minutes—ago. Daniel frequently drank himself into a stupor. If he did so today, Simon could well be here for the night.

The tavern door swung open. Daniel swaggered out, accompanied by a large man in the green and black tunic of Lord West's house. Daniel pointed toward the pillory. Simon closed his eyes and silently thanked a God he had never truly worshipped. It must be time for his release.

"There's the witch!" Daniel's voice cut through the sounds of the fair. Simon opened his eyes. Jessica stood before him, staring up with an angry expression. She raised her arms straight out from her sides. A blue light formed in the air in front of her, a sphere of power that crackled and spat like damp logs on a fire.

Simon tried to call out, to prevent her from casting whatever spell she planned, but could manage only a weak grunt. The whole village was here, watching. They might burn her immediately. The blue ball fizzed and burst with a soft pop. Jessica frowned, then a look of concentration crossed her face. Her arms tensed.

Daniel appeared behind her. He grabbed her arms and pulled them backwards. Jessica screamed and fought against him. Daniel forced her to her knees and twisted her arms so he could pin both of them behind her with one hand.

Jessica's hair covered her face as she struggled against his grip. The music stopped. People gathered in front of the pillory. With his free hand, Daniel slapped Jessica's head. She yelped, and stopped fighting. Daniel lifted her to her feet.

"Jessica Chadwick, I accuse you of witchcraft." Daniel took hold of her hair and pulled her head back. The crowd pressed forward.

"I saw her make blue fire in the air," called a voice from the back.

"She was going to kill Simon Bulcock," said another.

"Hang her before she kills us all," a woman's voice, high and trembling, sounded over the general hum of conversation. The murmur solidified into two words. "Hang her!"

Simon tried to speak. The effort made blood flow from the cut in his mouth.

"See! He bleeds! She did this." The murmurs of the crowd increased in intensity.

Simon shook his head. *No*, he wanted to shout. *Jessica tried to help me, not harm me. She has never hurt anyone.* He blinked and looked down into Jessica's eyes, saw the fear that shook her body, and tried again to speak. He only succeeded in making the blood flow faster from his mouth.

"Stop this." The man with Daniel, a burly, blond giant Simon recognized as Seth Crocker, climbed up beside the pillory. He held his arms high. "There are laws. She must have a trial. We will take her to Lord West and let him decide her fate."

"Laws be damned," shouted someone in the crowd. "We saw her try to kill Simon. Hang her now."

A white horse charged into the crowd, or so it seemed to Simon's exhausted eyes. Was it real, or just wishful thinking on his part? The screams of the crowd told him they saw it too. The horse reared, its eyes wide, its teeth bared. A runaway, panicked by the noise. Simon marveled that nobody had yet fallen under its hooves.

"Orobas! No!" Jessica shouted at the horse. The effect of her words was immediate. The horse stopped, its head lowered, and stared at her. She returned the stare, then the horse reared once more and ran back in the direction it had come.

Daniel tightened his grip. "She controls animals. We have all witnessed it. Seth is right, we must take her to Lord West, but I think we will have a hanging by tomorrow." He propelled Jessica away, toward the tavern. Seth jumped from the pillory and strode ahead of Daniel and Jessica to clear a path through the people.

Simon watched the procession through tear-blurred eyes. Jessica had performed magic in full view of the village, and she had indeed stopped the bolting horse. Simon let his head fall onto the inflexible support of the pillory, and wondered at the name Jessica had called the horse.

Orobas. A name he had seen before, somewhere. A name on a page, copied from a book. It was something he had forgotten, one of many things lost in the muddle of his mind. He closed his eyes and concentrated, thinking through red flashes of pain.

Chapter Sixteen

People pressed around Jessica and her captors, all of them jeering and shouting insults at her. One of them spat at her face. Jessica kept her head down and hoped Orobas had understood.

Jessica allowed Daniel and Seth to lead her to the cart beside the tavern. She made no attempt at resistance when they bound her hands and feet, and lay still in the back of the cart when they threw her in.

If she fought, it would give the men an excuse to beat her. If she managed to escape, the villagers would tear her apart. Jessica held back her fury and forced the trembling from her limbs. Once the cart was out of the village, she had only these two men with whom to contend. A simple unraveling spell would break her bonds, then, with luck, she might be able to jump from the cart and run into the woods.

The planks of the cart stank of manure. Jessica turned her face to her right to find Daniel squatted beside her. The cart lurched as Seth climbed onto the front. Daniel hauled Jessica into a sitting position and sat opposite her.

"You have not spoken, witch. Not one word in your own defense." He grasped the side rail as the cart jolted forward. "You do not deny the charge?"

Jessica clenched her teeth. There was nothing to gain by denial. Even if the village had not witnessed her magic, to deny an accusation of witchcraft was to invite the attentions of the torturer.

She was not going to give this man the satisfaction of a confession. Better to give him a demonstration. Jessica lowered her head so that her hair covered most of her face, then whispered the words of the unraveling.

"What are you doing there, witch?" Daniel moved closer. "Cursing us?"

Jessica stopped reciting the spell. The ropes around her wrists and ankles became less tight, their fibers partially separated from the effects of the spell, not yet enough to free herself, but she dared not risk Daniel's wrath.

If only she knew how to control the blue flare she had

accidentally used on Foras. When she had tried at the pillory, she had been unable to sustain the magic and the flare had dissipated. Her mother had told her, as had Foras, that her magic was unformed, untrained. She had produced only enough to condemn herself. Her apparent command of Orobas had made things worse.

"I asked you a question, witch." Daniel leaned forward and punched Jessica's shoulder. She ignored him.

After shouting Orobas's name, Jessica had remembered how Phenex had seen her thoughts, and wondered if Orobas could do the same. She pressed her thoughts forward and saw understanding in the horse-demon's eyes. By now, he should have returned to the house and told Foras and the others of her capture.

"Very well, if you don't want to speak to me, I'll make sure you don't speak at all." Daniel leaned over the front of the cart. "Seth, lend me your neck-scarf, would you?"

"What for?" Seth asked.

"I want to gag this witch. She's been muttering to herself, and I'm concerned she might be placing a curse on us."

Seth pulled his neck-scarf free and handed it to Daniel. "Make it tight, Dan. I don't want to be turned into a frog."

Laughing, Daniel twirled the cloth into a rope and tied it over Jessica's mouth. She gagged at the stale-sweat stench of the old scarf, but it was no worse than the manure stink of the cart. Jessica coughed and leaned back against the side rail. She would never get these smells out of her clothes.

The village was now out of sight, but Jessica could not recite her unraveling spell with the gag in her mouth. She had no choice but to hope for the intervention of the demons. Foras had said they must not interfere in human lives, nonetheless they must find a way to rescue her. If not for herself, then for the sake of their plan.

If these men, through their parody of justice, hanged her, there would be no need for the Witchfinder to come. The Golab would stay free, and all the demons' work would be in vain. She gazed back along the road, wondering if this was the last she would see of it.

A black cat emerged from the long grass beside the road, and stared at the cart. Jessica watched it recede into the distance. *Belson?* Something stretched from the grass, over the cat. Something long and thin, like a brown needle with joints. It snatched the cat back into the grass. Jessica sat up to get a better view, but Daniel pushed her back.

"Don't you be getting ideas, witch. Just sit there and wait until we get to Lord West's house. It won't be long."

"We're not taking her to the house." Seth turned in his seat to face Daniel. "We've all been told, if we find the witch, to take her to the tower."

Daniel's face paled. "The tower? Why?"

"Don't ask me. That's what Lord West told us all." Seth returned his attention to his horses. "I hear he's sent for the Witchfinder already."

Daniel slumped against the side of the cart. "So that's where Simon was going. Hell's hairy hands, I forgot about him when we caught this witch. He's long past his six hours for the day." He reached up and tapped Seth's back. "Seth, can I borrow your cart and horses, after we dispose of the witch? I have to get my prisoner out of the pillory."

"From what I've seen, you'll need to borrow me, too." Seth chuckled. "He won't be walking anywhere today. You'll need help to get him into the cart. Besides, where my horses go, I go."

Jessica stared from the back of the cart. Seth drove at barely more than walking pace, so the cart could not be disturbing the grass beside the road. Yet the grass on the right side of the road bent and dipped as though blown by a breeze. Jessica craned her neck, slowly so as not to draw Daniel's attention.

Something followed the cart, something hidden by the grass. Whatever it was, it was bigger and faster than Belson. She leaned toward the open rear of the cart in an attempt to catch a glimpse of what the thing might be.

"Oh, no you don't." Daniel pulled her backwards. "It won't do you any good anyway. Even if you fall out of the cart, you can't run with your legs tied." He brought his face close to hers. The ale and tobacco on his breath mixed with the manure and sweat stink in Jessica's nostrils. "You might kill yourself, and that would leave me and Seth in real trouble."

"Where she's going, she'd be better off dead." Seth glanced back at Jessica, a look of pity in his eyes.

Jessica looked from Seth to Daniel. Snatches of their conversation came back to her. They were taking her to a tower, but she knew of no towers nearby. It had been a long time since she saw Lord West's mansion, so maybe he had built one.

Seth had mentioned the Witchfinder. If he was on his way, then she had to get back to her house. Foras said the demons could not make the Golab visit the house. That was up to her. However, there was nothing she could do until she got rid of the gag.

"We're here." Seth stopped the cart outside a tower of black stone, a few hundred yards from Lord West's mansion. Gargoyles ringed the tower, but no windows broke the ebony smoothness of its walls.

Daniel shivered. "Let's be done, and be gone." He jumped from the cart, then turned and hauled Jessica across the boards. Seth lifted her in his arms and they approached the single door at the base of the tower.

Daniel knocked, then stepped back. Jessica wondered what could have possessed Lord West to build such a dark construction. With no windows it must be pitch black inside, yet the way Daniel knocked and waited suggested he expected to find someone in residence. Who could possibly want to live here?

The door swung inwards to reveal an interior as black as the outer walls. A stirring in the darkness resolved into the shape of a tall, thin man in a monk's habit. Jessica writhed in Seth's arms, staring at the figure in the doorway. Even the man's aura was black.

"Good afternoon, gentlemen." The voice from the monk's cowl was smooth and gentle, but its evil filled the air. "I see you have the witch. Bring her inside." The figure drifted back into the gloom of the tower.

Seth made a hesitant move forward. At Daniel's insistence, he took a few steps into the tower and laid Jessica on the floor. She tried to plead with him through her gag, but could make no intelligible sounds. Seth met her gaze for a moment and then retreated into the sunlight. The door closed.

Jessica lay in the silent darkness, hardly daring to breathe. She listened for a footfall, anything to tell her where the mysterious monk might be, but there was no sound at all.

A pale, sickly yellow light brightened slowly until it illuminated the room. Jessica could not determine its source. She lay on smooth black stone, surrounded by walls of the same material, in a room devoid of furniture. The junction between walls and floor was unclear, as if they melted into one another. The door through which she had entered became visible, as did a curved flight of stairs and three other doors opposite the first. The cowled figure stood a few feet away, his hands clasped.

"Ah, Jessica, I have waited so long to meet you." The figure drifted forward. "Let me dispense with your bonds, since it seems you lack the skill to do so yourself." He moved one hand in a slow arc through the air.

Jessica sat up. The ropes, and her gag, had vanished. Her unraveling spell would take time to work and would leave a pile of fibers from the ropes. She checked the floor, but there was no trace of dust. The man drifted closer. Jessica scrambled to her feet.

"Who are you? Witchfinder?" Jessica backed away. This man fitted no description of the Witchfinder she had heard, but his aura was stronger than a human's, and purely evil.

The figure stopped moving. A thin, wheezing laugh issued from the hood. "No, Jessica, I am not. I am a concerned friend. You may call me Nicholas."

"You are no friend of mine. I have never seen you before, nor do I wish to again." She ran for the door.

"Leaving so soon?" Nicholas made no move to stop her as she grabbed the door handle. Jessica pulled, but the door stood solid. She looked down at the handle to see if there was some kind of latch, and screamed. The handle was made of flesh; warm, raw and bleeding. Jumping back, Jessica rubbed her hand on her skirt. She screamed again as Demdike appeared beside her.

"It is illusion, my dear. There is nothing to fear. Calm yourself. I prefer not to harm you. We have business to discuss."

"What business? I want nothing to do with you."

"I advise you to reconsider. I have already saved your life. It is now mine to do with as I will."

"What do you mean?" Jessica leaned against the wall beside the door.

"There were soldiers, intent on denouncing you as a witch. I prevented it."

Jessica checked her hands and dress, but found no blood on them. The door handle was now brass, gleaming in the yellow light. She pursed her lips. Simon had mentioned soldiers. Nicholas said he had stopped them.

"Why? What do you want with me?"

"I want to train you. I want you to join your power with mine. You contain potent magic, as did your mother. As did others before her. You have been told of your great-aunt, who was known as Chattox?"

"She was evil, as are you. I want no part of any business you may propose."

"So you have said. There is no need to waste breath on repetition. Better to wait until you have something new to say." Nicholas moved past her, the odor of decay following his movement like an invisible cloud. "Your great-aunt had a partner, you know."

"No. I didn't know. What of it?"

"Your great-aunt's partner was my daughter. She married, but she was often called by her maiden name. You have not heard it?"

Jessica shook her head. Every breath she inhaled filled her with more of Nicholas's stench. "It's not possible. You would be a hundred years old."

"I stopped counting at a hundred and twenty. Birthdays become something of a chore after that." Nicholas waved his hand in a dismissive gesture. "You must hear the name of your great-aunt's partner. She was called Demdike." Beneath the cowl, Nicholas's mouth separated into a smile. Yellow, pointed teeth glistened between cracked blue lips. "I was her father."

"Your name is Demdike? Then it was you who sent my mother to the flames." Jessica searched her mind for any clue as to how she might form her blue flare.

"That is what your father suspected, but you should hear the truth of it from Simon Bulcock. I don't wonder that he has concealed his guilt in this."

"No. I won't hear it. You are trying to blame Simon for your own guilt. I heard your name from my mother's own lips. You are the one responsible for her death." Caught between fear and fury, Jessica could not concentrate on her magic. If she tried to use her power on Demdike, she might fail, and she did not know how he might retaliate. She slid along the wall, toward the stairs.

Demdike sighed. His breath expelled a cloud of ash. "Ah, this is unfortunate. I should have brought you here before you called your mother. An oversight on my part. Your power developed faster than I had anticipated."

He placed his hands together and interlocked his fingers. "Let us not dwell on the past, Jessica. I offer you a partnership. Together, our powers will be impenetrable. I urge you to think quickly. The Witchfinder has been summoned. With my help, you can defeat him. Alone, you will hang."

"You are a monster."

Demdike cackled. "I am human, though a little improved. Consider carefully, Jessica. If you fight me, you will die at the hands of the Witchfinder. If you join me, he will die."

"The Witchfinder would hang us both. You are a fool to call him here."

"He is coming." Demdike shrugged. "He will not see through my magic. I will entrance him, as I have everyone else. He will believe I have always been here as advisor to the puny Lord West."

He doesn't know what the Witchfinder really is, Jessica thought. *He thinks he will be dealing with a human.*

Jessica folded her arms and squared her shoulders. Demdike had no hope of destroying the Golab. Unless, perhaps, his magic had grown to demonic proportions. It was possible. He had clearly cheated death with his power. No, an alliance with a creature so evil was unthinkable. Her best chance lay with Foras and the other demons. She had to stall for time until she could escape and lead the Witchfinder back to her house.

"I have to think about this. Will you let me return home?"

"You may think all you wish, but you must do it here." Demdike made a sign with his fingers and Jessica's arms flew back against the wall. Manacles appeared on her wrists and ankles. Chains embedded themselves in the wall behind her.

Demdike moved toward the door. "The Witchfinder will arrive tomorrow. You have until then. Now, I must inform my little pet Lord of your capture, or he is likely to have another of his tantrums."

Demdike opened the door and moved out into the lengthening afternoon shadows, leaving Jessica to pull at her chains. The yellow light faded from the room. If she could not escape her only hope of defeating the Golab would be to surrender to Demdike, to darkness more complete than that surrounding her now.

Chapter Seventeen

Simon spent eight hours in the pillory. If there was justice in the world, he would have to suffer only four hours tomorrow. He sighed. There was no justice, in this world, or the next, for the likes of him.

The iron manacles bit into his aching wrists, their flesh swollen and bleeding from Daniel's ropes. If that sot had done his job, Simon would have been resting in the barn two hours earlier. The chains on his arms were too short to allow him to lie down, but at least he could sit on the straw-covered floor and rest his legs.

There was no escape from the pressure in his face, no matter how he adjusted the position of his head. The swelling in his cheek felt as though it would burst, and his tongue filled his mouth so that it hurt even to breathe.

He tried to talk to Daniel, to ask about Jessica, to tell him what he knew of Demdike. Daniel had ignored Simon's grunts and half-formed words. Without speech, there was nothing more Simon could do. If he could, he would have laughed at the thought.

He had nothing left to do, no friends left to betray. Jessica had, in the end, betrayed herself when she showed her magic in the village square. No, he could not pass the blame so easily. She was doomed from the moment he told Demdike her name.

What did blame matter now? Even if the soldiers killed Demdike, the villagers were now certain to hang Jessica for the animals Demdike had mutilated. The Witchfinder would silence any dissenting voices among them. Simon alone knew the truth. He alone had the words that might sway them, might persuade them not to kill. He now had no voice for those words.

The last rays of the Mayday sun filtered through the gaps in the barn door. Light faded from the world as the land settled into gloom and waited for the rise of the waning moon. The night chill drifted through the barn, whispering in the straw to wake the scurrying creatures, the mice, rats and spiders, and send them about their evening business.

Simon shifted in the straw, trying to avoid the cold breeze. A rustle beside him, followed by an angry chittering, told him he disturbed one of the barn's permanent residents. Simon ignored the sound. The mice, or maybe even rats, held no terrors for him. They were unlikely to trouble him. He smelled worse than they did.

He found the least painful position for his arms and settled himself for the night. Though exhausted, he resisted sleep, fearful of what dreams might visit him in the darkness.

A creaking sound accompanied a blast of cold air. Simon looked up and forgot his pain for a moment. He struggled to his feet to face his visitor. The dark outline in the doorway could belong to only one man.

"Ah, Simon. Good to see you can still stand." Demdike moved forwards until he stood a few feet from Simon, the hem of his cloak rustling on the straw.

Life was crap, but it was all he had left. Simon quaked in terror at the thought of ending it here, chained like an animal in a filthy barn. He turned his gaze to the floor, so he would not see the killing blow when it came.

"You seem frightened. There's no need. Your capture was not your fault. There will be no punishment for that."

"Uh?" Simon looked up, into the hooded face before him. He had never seen Demdike's eyes, but he fancied he could now. There, in the shadow of the cowl, where eyes should be, were two patches of black, darker than the darkness surrounding them. Simon blinked, wondering how black could glow.

"My errand has been accomplished. It was done faster than you could have achieved it. So you need not fear on that point." Demdike lifted one hand and inspected his fingers. "There is, however, the matter of the soldiers you sent to my home. For that, I will punish you." Demdike bared his teeth. "First, I will hear your explanation for this treachery."

"Uh." Simon could make no other sound.

"Are you incapable of speech?" Demdike leaned forward. His corpse-like odor assaulted Simon's nostrils. "I see that you are. Well, I have never enjoyed the tedium of one-sided conversations." Demdike pressed his fingers into Simon's swollen cheek and jaw.

Lights burst behind Simon's eyes. Every muscle in his body tensed against the agony that seared his face. He closed his eyes and tried not to visualize Demdike's fingers probing, penetrating his cheek, reaching for his tongue.

Demdike withdrew his hand. "That will do. I will leave you with some discomfort. You deserve no less."

"Ah." Simon moved his jaw. It hurt, but it moved. His tongue still felt large, but no longer pressed against the roof of his mouth. "I can speak." The words slurred, but they were words. "Thank you, Master Demdike."

"I do not want gratitude. I want an explanation."

"Jessica." Simon turned his eyes back to the floor. "They will hang her. You planned to let her take the blame for the animals you killed."

"Animals?" Demdike inclined his head. "Ah, I see you made the connection between the soldiers you saw and the animals. Yes, I took parts from the animals—items I needed for my work. You have jumped to an irrational conclusion, Simon. I have never intended for Jessica to die at the hands of the Witchfinder. I have called him here as a bargaining tool. Insurance, you might say, in case she proved difficult to convince."

"You did not plan her death?"

"Her magic is more useful to me if she is alive." Demdike sniffed. "So it was a misunderstanding. That is not an excuse I will accept. Four more soldiers are dead because of your hasty, half-witted deduction. Soldiers who were seen in the village. Many people know they came to visit me." Demdike rubbed his chin. "Such interference adds an unwelcome complication to my work."

"I am sorry, Master Demdike. Sometimes my thoughts are not my own, it seems. I am often confused, as though I have two minds." Simon looked up. "Daniel Featherstone has captured Jessica. He has taken her to Lord West for trial. You must help her."

"Jessica is safely within my grasp now, despite your incompetence. I had hoped to do things differently but my ends will still be achieved." Demdike tapped his teeth with one of his long, blackened fingernails. "I should kill you now, but that will only complicate matters further. The villagers are already anxious. A sudden death will not go unnoticed and for some inexplicable reason, you are popular with them."

He pointed his finger at Simon's nose. "If you wish to live beyond tomorrow, you will keep silent. You must tell nobody else what you know. Remember, I have yet to decide on your punishment. It may be easy, it may not. Keep silent and I might forget to punish you at all."

"Thank you, Master Demdike." Simon bowed his head. "What will happen to Jessica?"

"She is in my care. You need concern yourself with no more than that. You, Simon, are my servant. You will do as you are told, no more and no less. If you feel you should speak out, or disagree with my commands, think of the soldiers you saw."

"I understand." Simon knew he could not fight Demdike, even if he were not chained and exhausted. Better to agree, to survive, to find a way to fight tomorrow.

"Good. When you have served your time in the pillory, visit me. I will give you instruction in the things you must do to avoid my punishment." Demdike retreated to the door. Simon looked up in time to see it close, although Demdike had already vanished.

Simon settled back into the straw and wept for Jessica. Even if she survived the Witchfinder and the fury of the village, Demdike planned to corrupt her to his cruel ways. If she escaped both Demdike and the Witchfinder, the villagers would kill her for the crimes they imagined she had committed.

There was only one hope. Jessica had to escape from the village and hide somewhere else. A different name, a different town, where nobody would find her. It had to be done tomorrow or it would be too late. By tomorrow night, Jessica would be either dead or corrupted.

A cramp ached in his left leg. Simon moved, and the iron manacles cut into his wrists. He gasped at the pain. His hands were curled into numb claws. Today's injuries would take weeks to fully heal, and there was more to come tomorrow. Somehow, Simon had to convince Daniel of Jessica's innocence, but Daniel had witnessed Jessica's command of the horse. He would not be easily swayed.

Orobas. That was the name she had used. Why did it sound familiar? Once more, he saw the mental image of Lord West's land, with a green space where Demdike's tower should be. Simon had told Demdike the truth. He often felt as though he had two minds. One of these minds must know the answers to his questions.

Simon fought back pain, defied the exhaustion pulling at his eyelids, ignored the hunger that writhed in his guts, and took himself into his own mind. It was a difficult feat, one Demdike had taught him in early lessons, and one he had never fully mastered.

Images flashed on his inner eye, thoughts and ideas drifted on turbulent seas of memory. Everything was chaos, as though a finger had probed his brain and stirred, leaving his memories a shambles. Simon caught one of the images and held it still, a point of reference in the madness of his mind.

It was Elizabeth, leading him away from Chattox's group under a cloak of power. The old crone Chattox was blind, but nothing was ever hidden from her magic. Elizabeth had saved him just as the people of the town arrived to take Chattox and her group away. Under Elizabeth's protection, he had passed unseen from the remote house and had escaped the gallows that awaited the captured witches.

Something hid in the shadows of that memory. Something about another woman, a friend of Chattox who shared her evil ways. Simon could not recall that name but it was one Elizabeth had mentioned often.

If only Elizabeth were here now. She would know what to do. Simon let the image go. If Elizabeth were here she might kill him for the things he had done.

Another image came to him, one he did not remember. Elizabeth again, this time dressed in white and smiling at him.

"Simon," she said.

Simon gasped. He had never delved so far into this procedure before. Was it normal for memories to speak?

"You did not betray me. Look." Elizabeth moved aside. Behind her formed the image of an ale-house Simon had once frequented. At one of the rough-hewn tables, an upset tankard beside him was Simon. His eyes were glazed, his mouth worked but no sound came out. Behind the image stood Nicholas Demdike in his monk's cowl. He leaned over the insensible Simon and spoke to two men seated opposite him.

Elizabeth came into view again. The image faded behind her. "You see? Demdike led you to believe that you gave my name to those men, but you were too drunk to remember. It was him, not you, who gave me to the executioners."

"It can't be." Simon heard his own voice echo in his mind. "How can I recall things that happened when I was all but unconscious?"

"These are not your memories. These are visions of the past." Elizabeth took a step closer. "You have moved within yourself, as I taught you, to the place between life and death."

"Nicholas taught me this. An aid to concentration."

"That creature taught you nothing." Elizabeth wore an expression of disgust. "He has manipulated your memories, disordered your mind. As he has the rest of this village, with the exception of my Jessica. She is free of his control, thanks to you."

"Me? All I have done is to bring disaster on my friends."

"You isolated her. She was never infected by Demdike's

influence. You, and the others, all believe his tower to be ancient. Think hard on that, Simon, because you are wrong. I see the first stirrings of doubt in your mind. I will help you, but you must help Jessica in return. Save her from Demdike."

"I will, and from the Witchfinder also."

Elizabeth laughed. "For that, she has sufficient help already, I think."

Simon wanted to reach out, to touch his old friend, to apologize for giving her husband to the Roundheads. In this place, he had no physical presence. Elizabeth faded from view. A shockwave rocked his thoughts at her passing.

His two minds became one. He remembered Elizabeth's teachings, recalled Demdike claiming them as his own. Simon remembered Nicholas Demdike's attempts to persuade Elizabeth to leave her group to follow him, her furious denouncement of him and his threats to break her family. A page appeared—a possession of Elizabeth's, copied from a book with a name and a description. Orobas, the fifty-fifth spirit of the Goetia. Simon's inner self glowed with relief. Jessica had a demon on her side.

There was a thought, a snatch of remembered conversation, which had long been denied his waking thoughts. It surfaced, bubbling through the mire Demdike had piled into his brain.

It was Seth Crocker's voice, muttering through his beer in the tavern, not long after Matthew Chadwick and the others were taken by Cromwell's army. Matthew should not have been in the field that day. Lord West had given orders that he be moved, from tending the dairy herd to planting the field.

Simon opened his eyes to the chill reality of the barn. He accepted the pain, the hunger and exhaustion. Cold air cut at his skin, and he relished the sensation, blind to all but vengeance in his fury.

It was Demdike who betrayed Elizabeth.

It must have been Demdike who arranged for Matthew Chadwick to be pressed into the army.

All this time, Simon had blamed himself, but it was never his fault. Demdike had, as he promised, destroyed Elizabeth's family and had let Simon accept the guilt. With both parents gone, all that stood between Demdike and Jessica was Simon, and he was already in Demdike's thrall. There was more, much more. The filthy mud with which Demdike had blocked Simon's thoughts now dried and fell apart.

Those memories, the terror of childhood when he and his

friends had dared each other to touch the tower. Conversations with Demdike, reaching back decades. They were all illusion. There had been no tower on Lord West's property when Simon was younger. His Lordship had been a strong man—not physically, but morally.

The tower appeared when Demdike arrived. When His Lordship became reclusive, mean and spiteful. When the punishments for trespass and poaching increased in cruelty. When Daniel, once his friend, became his enemy. Simon remembered.

The tower had appeared overnight, as had Demdike. Three years ago. Simon saw it arrive, as he passed on his poaching rounds. Demdike drew him in, made a servant of him, filled his mind with false memories.

Simon was the first, followed within a day by the rest of the village. He recalled the night Demdike's tower landed, borne by a giant creature with bat's wings. It was the night before the first mutilated animals had been found.

Chapter Eighteen

"It's bigger inside than out."

"Quiet. We have no time for sightseeing."

The low voices, the first high-pitched and sibilant, the second deep and powerful, came from somewhere in the room, but Jessica could see nothing. She held herself still, listening, hoping to remain unnoticed.

"I was just saying. It's not like Malphas's work. Too dark, too miserable. Malphas likes windows."

"Quiet, Bifrons, or I'll step on you."

Jessica sighed in relief. The voices must be the two demons Orobas mentioned. She shifted her weight and the chains jingled with her movement.

"There she is. Make some light, Bifrons. Not too much, don't turn this place into a lighthouse."

A feeble white globe appeared in the air near the middle of the room. It brightened gradually until most of the centre of the room was visible, although the corners remained in shadow. The light revealed a tall, heavyset man standing a few feet from Jessica. He was dressed all in white, and his bearded face wore a kindly smile.

Jessica returned the smile, unable to fully believe this gentle giant could be a demon. Her smile faded as something scuttled away from the tall man's feet and darted for the shadows in the alcove that led to the stairs.

"What was that?" Jessica pulled against her chains, trying to see where the little creature had gone. It seemed to be about the size of a small dog, but the way it moved was unlike any animal she had seen before.

"That was Bifrons. It's best he keeps out of sight for now. My name is Seere. We are taking you home." Seere inspected her chains as he spoke.

"You can't break those chains, Seere. If you do, he'll know." Bifrons spoke from the shadows, his sibilant voice accentuating every 's'.

"Then I will take her out of them." Seere stepped back and pointed a thick finger at Jessica. He closed his eyes for a moment, then turned and pointed at a spot in the middle of the floor.

"There."

The world turned upside down and inside out. Jessica gasped for breath and fought nausea as the room became a maelstrom of colors and shapes, none of which she could identify.

She had a fleeting glimpse of the manacles passing through her wrists. The vision stopped as abruptly as it had started. She stood in the centre of the room, facing the empty manacles that now dangled from the wall.

"How...?" The question died on her lips when Bifrons shot out of the shadows. He was a head; bald, wrinkled and ruddy, with two small arms protruding from just beneath his ears. At his neck, eight spider legs spread out, tapping the flagstones in a rapid tattoo as he ran toward her. His grin showed thin, needle-sharp teeth.

A heavy hand clamped over Jessica's mouth before she could scream. Seere's other arm encircled her waist and lifted her. She writhed in his grip as Bifrons arrived at her feet.

"Good evening, witch. You are prettier than Foras described." The spider legs clattered in a dance.

"Bifrons, you have neither tact nor diplomacy. Your appearance terrifies humans, yet you seem not to notice." Chastisement mingled with amusement in Seere's tone.

"We are not all gifted with pretty bodies, Seere. I make the best of what I have. My other form is difficult to hold for long." Bifrons scratched above his ear with one short arm. His leering grin never left his face.

Jessica stopped struggling but kept her gaze on the freakish monstrosity before her. The hands holding her relaxed a little as Seere lowered her to the ground.

"Make no sound." He spoke close to her ear as he released his hand from her mouth. "Bifrons is not the monster he appears to be. He will help you, not harm you."

Heavy hooves sounded on the flagstones as a huge white horse stepped from the air. It was as though the animal simply walked from behind some unseen barrier. Jessica's eyes widened.

"Orobas?" She took a step toward the horse, but instead of Orobas's brown eyes, this horse stared at her with eyes of bright sky-blue. There were no pupils, no whites at the corners, just pure blue orbs.

"This is my horse. His name cannot be pronounced by voices as limited as yours." Seere carried Jessica to it and set her on its back. "I can twist space, but only around myself. My horse can travel within and between the spaces I form."

Jessica grabbed the horse's mane. It turned its head and snickered at her.

"Loosen your grip. He will not let you fall." Seere climbed up behind her, lifting Bifrons as he did so. He placed Bifrons in front of Jessica. She immediately released the horse's mane and pressed herself back into Seere. Bifrons leered up at her, waggling his eyebrows. He reached out one thin leg and lifted her skirt.

Biting her lip, Jessica pressed her skirt down. Bifrons withdrew his leg and pouted.

"Bifrons. Behave yourself." Seere's chuckle shook him, overwhelming the tremble in Jessica's body. A strong arm encircled her waist once more. "You need not fear Bifrons. His lusty manner is an empty threat. He no longer has the equipment to carry it through."

Jessica moved her head to speak to Seere, but kept watching the grinning Bifrons. "Where is Orobas? I thought this horse was him."

"Orobas is at the trap. Your house, I mean. He is too excitable for such subtle work." Seere smiled at her. "Best close your eyes. Too much of this can drive a mortal insane."

Seere spoke a few words in some guttural tongue. Jessica closed her eyes, though that did nothing to help the knots that formed in her stomach as Seere's spell took effect.

"We have arrived." Seere's heavy hands lifted Jessica from the horse. She opened her eyes as her feet touched soft ground.

Foras stood before her, bathed in the light of the moon. Beneath them was the short-cropped grass of the garden, and ahead was the rear of her house. Jessica's head still spun from the ride on Seere's horse.

She narrowed her eyes. The house looked different in moonlight. It looked larger. She wondered how many rooms Malphas had added today. She blinked, and ran her gaze along the circle of windows surrounding the garden, trying to find stability in their solid presence.

Some distance away, in the centre of the circle, a bird swooped and dived at the stone block she had seen earlier. Even at that distance—almost a quarter of a mile—the bird looked huge. It glowed flame-red, with a golden aura and it was carving—rather it was melting—the stone of the block. At each pass, the bird shot flame at the stone, then backed away as though to inspect the result.

Jessica turned to Foras. "What—I mean, who is that?"

"That is Phenex. You have met."

"Phenex? But he was a little boy." Jessica looked back at the magnificent bird.

Foras sighed. "Many of us can assume different forms, each within our own abilities. We will not be able to permanently assume our true forms unless we return to the Host. That is our mission, which must be performed with care."

The last words were harsh, and directed not at Jessica, but at Seere and Bifrons. "You were not to interfere unless her life was in danger."

Bifrons folded his arms. "We cannot interfere in the normal lives of mortals. We did not."

"You released her from the necromancer's home, when he was absent."

"Oh, that hardly counts as interference. Besides, he is not a mortal." Bifrons raised both his eyebrows, half-closed his eyes and tilted his head back.

"What?" Jessica stared down at Bifrons. "He said he was human."

"Ah, yes he was, once, but he's not now. Not completely. He just thinks he is." Bifrons looked away, a smug expression on his face.

"You speak in riddles, Bifrons. Be plain. Tell us what you know." Foras knelt in the grass beside the little demon.

"Bifrons recognized the necromancer." Seere said. "He is Nicholas Demdike."

"Demdike!" Foras shot to his feet, grabbed Jessica's arm and pulled her toward the house. Seere and Bifrons followed.

"You know this Demdike?" Jessica struggled to keep pace. "What is he?"

Foras stopped moving. His jaw jutted, his lips formed a scowl. "He is the worst thing that could happen now. Demdike is a pawn of Baal. He has bargained for many years, hoping to become one of Baal's *Harab-Serapel*." He paused. "A Raven of Death. If he learns of our activities here he will certainly inform Baal, who will find it amusing to inform Asmodeus." Foras resumed his hasty retreat to the house, dragging Jessica with him.

Foras released her as they entered the hallway. "Orobas! Marchosias! Amon! Malphas!" He called the names as he strode around the floor, opening doors and calling up the stairs.

Malphas appeared first, hopping down the stairs, followed by Orobas. "What is it, Foras? You sound distressed." Malphas faced Foras, while Orobas moved to Jessica's side. He dipped his long head so that he could look into her eyes.

"You are safe. Good. I could not help you in the village without revealing myself."

"I'm glad you didn't." Jessica managed a brief smile. "They would have killed me there and then." She patted Orobas's arm. For a moment, he seemed more like a pet horse than a powerful demon.

Amon slithered from the new door that led to Jessica's garden, while a large black wolf appeared from the opposite door. Folded along the wolf's back was a pair of feathered wings, and his tail was covered in scales like a viper's. Jessica found she could accept this without question. If she could accept Bifrons, she could face anything.

"You called?" The wolf barked the words.

"Marchosias. Amon. You have had dealings with Baal in the past. Do you remember a mortal named Nicholas Demdike?"

"Yes, a particularly nasty soul. Surely he must be dead by now. That was a very long time ago." Amon slithered closer.

"He wished to become *Harab-Serapel*." Marchosias laughed. "As if Baal would ever allow it."

"He lives." Foras stood, hands on hips. "He is here. Bifrons, Seere, tell them what you saw."

As Seere recounted their visit to Demdike's tower and Jessica's rescue, the demons huddled closer. Bifrons interrupted with details where Seere missed them. Jessica stood outside their circle, close enough to hear what was said. Malphas held up his wing.

"This tower. Did it have windows?"

"None that we saw." Seere shook his head.

"Aha, then it is the work of Sabnock. He builds gloomy places, no natural light illuminates his toils."

Foras shook his head. "Does it matter?"

"Perhaps." Malphas turned his beak to Foras. "Sabnock's towers are mobile. They can be transported from one place to another in an instant, usually with the help of Gaap. This Demdike may disappear at any moment, if the whim takes him."

"He won't." Jessica took a step back as all the demons turned to face her. "He wants me to join him, because of my magic." She took a deep breath and paused to stop the tremble in her lip. "It was Demdike who gave my mother to the executioners. My father told me. Now he wants me. He has called the Witchfinder here, and if I don't accept his terms, he will name me as a witch." She swallowed hard and blinked away a tear. "I think he must have tried the same thing with my mother, but she refused him. So he let them burn her."

"Then we must deal with him." Foras sighed. He placed his hand on her shoulder and squeezed, then spoke to Orobas.

"Orobas, how likely is it that Demdike will become *Harab-Serapel*?"

"Not likely. As Marchosias said, Baal would not allow it. He plays with Demdike. He encourages this necromancer to commit atrocities in the hope he will one day attain Baal's favor. Baal keeps him alive as a toy, an entertaining distraction."

Orobas ran his hand through his mane. "However, if Baal finds out what we are doing, he might transform Demdike to thwart our plans. It would amuse him."

Marchosias flexed his wings. "The Hiding is in place. We can work around this Demdike. He is no threat to us unless Baal learns of our plans."

"Not so." Orobas tapped his fingers together. "Demdike is powerful. Not enough to threaten us, but certainly enough to harm Jessica. He will try to take her for himself before the Golab arrives."

Jessica coughed. "He wants to kill the Witchfinder."

All eyes were on her again. Foras spoke in a low voice. "Does he know?"

"No. He thinks the Witchfinder is just a man."

Foras rubbed his neck. "He will fail, but he might kill its host and set it loose. If the Golab enters Demdike, it will have access to his powers. That will make things awkward."

All the demons started talking at once. Jessica caught snatches of their conversation, and what she heard chilled her. The ferocity of the Golab with the powers of a necromancer like Demdike would be a formidable enemy indeed. She shivered. Foras noticed her, and called for silence. He took her aside as the babble of voices rose again.

"Go to sleep, Jessica. You will need all your strength. I think this might prove more difficult than we had thought." He led her to the stairs.

"Sleep, Foras? I have met the man who caused my mother's death. Tomorrow I risk my own life to catch the Witchfinder. How can I sleep?" Jessica stared into Foras's face, fascinated by the green glow of his eyes, and hoping he would offer to accompany her.

Foras pursed his lips. "Bifrons knows how to still the mind. I could send him with you."

"No." Jessica pulled away. She had accepted Bifrons as essentially friendly, but the thought of being alone with the lust-filled spider demon horrified her. What might he get up to once she fell asleep? "No, I will manage. I have a sleep spell of my own. I've used it before, to help me find rest when my father was taken." She hurried up the stairs.

At the top, she looked back. The demons huddled in their circle, their urgent chatter incomprehensible now. Foras stood at the bottom of the staircase, his face full of concern. He smiled and waved her away. At his feet, Bifrons waved also, and gave an exaggerated wink.

Chapter Nineteen

Seth Crocker climbed from his cart and joined Daniel Featherstone at the door to the barn.

"Think he'll still be alive?" Seth's words made Daniel hesitate with his hand on the door.

"Don't talk like that, Seth. He won't die so easily. Simon's a tough old bugger." Daniel pulled the door open. Simon sat motionless on the straw, his head forward, gray hair hiding his face.

"Oh, hell." Seth took a hesitant step forward. Simon's hands, visible in the manacles that held them, were blue. "Dan, you left him too long yesterday."

"Don't blame me for this." Daniel walked to Simon and nudged him with his boot. "Blame the witch. If not for her, he'd have been out of the pillory sooner."

Simon groaned. Seth rushed forward and lifted Simon's head.

"He's alive, but only just. Get these chains off him, Dan, and let's take him outside." Seth rolled his sleeves back, almost to his shoulders. Simon was filthy, and skin was easier to wash than cloth.

Daniel fumbled with a metal hoop bearing a few keys, found the right one and unlocked the manacles on Simon's wrists. Seth lifted the limp man and carried him out to his cart. He laid Simon gently onto the back of the cart, then pushed the man's hair aside to see his face. Daniel stood alongside Seth.

"Looks like the swelling's gone down in his mouth, anyway." Daniel wrinkled his nose. "He doesn't smell any better though."

"Neither would you, in his place." Seth picked up one of Simon's hands and examined it. "Cold and stiff. I bet he won't be doing any poaching for a long time."

"That's the idea." Daniel puffed out his chest. "He'll learn his lesson. Don't poach where Daniel Featherstone is bailiff."

Seth gritted his teeth. He had agreed to help Daniel move Simon this morning so that he could keep an eye on the bailiff. He knew Daniel was capable of cruelty, and from what he had seen of Simon the previous day, he doubted the poacher had the strength to withstand Daniel's application of punishment.

"There's a flagon of small beer in the front of my cart, and a tarpaulin under the seat. Go get them, Dan."

Daniel hesitated. "Now, don't you start bossing me around, Seth Crocker. There's an order to things, you know."

"Dan, for God's sake. Just get them." Seth faced Daniel, fists clenched. The muscles in his bare arms tensed. Seth stood taller than Daniel, and wider at the shoulders though not at the waist. Unlike Daniel, Seth's bulk was muscle, not fat.

"Okay, I'll get them." Daniel hurried to the front of the cart. "I'm just saying, don't start giving orders where you've no right. You don't want to fall foul of Lord West's justice yourself."

I'll rip that pillory from the ground and beat you to death with it if you try anything. Seth kept his thoughts to himself for now. Daniel was bearable most of the time, but occasionally his arrogance became too much for Seth's patience. He snatched the stone flagon from Daniel, pulled out the cork and lifted Simon's head with one hand.

Simon spluttered at the beer trickling over his lips. His chest shuddered with a deep breath. Seth waited a moment then raised the flagon to Simon's lips once more.

"Take it slow, Simon. A little at a time." Seth persisted until Simon had managed a few mouthfuls, then he lowered Simon's head back to the boards of the cart.

Daniel had dropped the tarpaulin beside Simon and now leaned against the side of the cart with his pipe in his hand. Seth grabbed the tarpaulin, shook it out and spread it over Simon.

"Don't be all day, Seth. He has a date with the pillory."

"You're not serious, Dan?" Seth pulled a corner of the tarpaulin, folded it and slipped it under Simon's head. "He's near enough dead now. He can't stand in the pillory today."

"Lord West's orders." Daniel puffed his pipe alight. "Two days."

"Forget it. He needs help, and I'll see he gets it."

"What? Are you turning against his Lordship?" Daniel gave Seth a sly look. "That pillory will be a tight fit for you, Seth."

"Don't threaten me. Better to look to yourself, when the village finds out what you've done to Simon. He's well liked there."

Daniel snorted. "Don't I know it. All day in the pillory, and not so much as a cabbage thrown at him. Apart from those soldiers." Daniel sucked at his pipe. "I wonder what happened to them."

"Who cares?" Seth flexed his arms to give Daniel a good view of his muscles. Seth had never been one for prolonged debates. A show of strength usually finished any argument involving him. "I say Simon needs help, not punishment, today."

"Two days." Daniel raised his eyebrows at Seth's pumped-up muscles. "Although, I suppose it need not be two consecutive days. I can wait until he is fit to stand." Daniel inspected the toe of his boot.

"Good enough." Seth moved to the front of the cart. "You'd better get in the back with Simon. Give him beer if he needs it." Seth climbed into his seat, picked up the reins then looked over his shoulder. "A sip at a time. Don't drown him." He set the cart moving at a slow pace to avoid bumping Simon around too much.

The road from the barn passed between Lord West's house and Demdike's tower. Muffled shouting echoed from the far side of the tower as they approached.

"What's all that?" Daniel sat up in the back of the cart. "Something's going on."

"Sounds like trouble at Demdike's door." Seth kept his eyes on the tower as the cart rolled forward.

Daniel sniffed. "Well, let him sort it out. I don't feel inclined to help that black-hearted old devil. Besides, I have a prisoner to escort."

The door at the base of the tower came into view. Demdike stood in his doorway, his face covered by his hood and his hands clasped at his chest. Three men faced him. One of them, a short man in the tall hat, cape, and tight leggings of a city gentleman, shouted abuse at Demdike.

The other two wore less expensive clothes, though all three were dressed in the simple black and white of the Puritan. Between them, these two men held three horses, all of which pulled at their reins as though desperate to escape.

Daniel shifted to get a better view. "That must be the Witchfinder," he whispered. "Sounds like he's furious about something."

Seth nodded. He watched the city man's rant from the corner of his eye as he coaxed his horses past the scene. "He's using some strong language for a pious man. There's words coming out of him I haven't even heard in the tavern."

Daniel gave a low whistle. "Old Demdike isn't used to being spoken to like that. We'd best be on our way quick, Seth. This is going to put Demdike in a foul temper."

"Hoi. You there." The Witchfinder called to Seth. "Stop. Stop, I say."

Seth pulled back on the reins. The cart halted. Seth kept

his gaze on his horses as the Witchfinder and the Puritans approached. They stopped a few feet from Seth's cart. Seth risked a glance in their direction. The Witchfinder's horses seemed calmer at this distance from Demdike.

"You look like healthy, God-fearing men." The Witchfinder spoke directly to Seth. "Unlike that useless stick-man in the tower. We have traveled a long way to see the Lord's work done, and the fool has let the witch escape."

Seth pushed his chin into his chest. He could not let these men see his smirk. Seth had spent a restless night wondering if he had done the right thing in taking Jessica to Demdike. They were his orders, and he had obeyed them. Still, the news that she had escaped Demdike's clutches relieved him. Witch she may be, but she had done no harm that he knew of.

"What?" Daniel jumped from the cart and walked up to the men. "After all the trouble we had catching her?"

"You are the very ones who caught her?" The Witchfinder smiled at Daniel. "Then you are indeed soldiers of the Lord. Perhaps you can assist me further."

"We have to get this man some help. He is dying." Seth jerked his thumb at the back of the cart. As if on cue, Simon groaned.

"It will take a moment of your time, no more." The Witchfinder stepped forward.

"Whatever help we can give, we will." Daniel hooked his thumbs into his jerkin. "And be proud to give it."

The Witchfinder held out his hand to Daniel. "It is good to meet honest men in these times. I am Matthew Hopkins, Witchfinder-General."

Daniel shook Hopkins' hand. "Daniel Featherstone, bailiff." He inclined his head toward Seth. "This is Seth Crocker, cartman for Lord West. How can we be of service?"

Simon groaned again. Seth looked back. "Dan, we have little time if we are to save this man's life." Seth doubted Simon would die, but something about Hopkins unnerved him. There was also Demdike, who watched them from his doorway. Seth's hands itched to flick the reins and get his horses moving.

"I have only one question." Hopkins faced Daniel. "The withered idiot in the tower could not, or would not tell us where the witch might have gone. She must have a home. Do either of you know where it is?"

Seth opened his mouth to say no, but Daniel spoke first. "Certainly. She has a cottage, beside the road that runs through the woods. I can direct you."

Seth closed his eyes while Daniel gave directions to Jessica's house. It would be better if this Witchfinder left without his kill. It would be better still if he took Demdike with him. Daniel, too. Daniel was an old friend, but his powers as bailiff had gone to his head.

Seth furrowed his brow. Daniel had not always been this way, he was sure. He had always been arrogant and self-centered, but this cruelty, this willingness to participate in the suffering of others, was a new side of Daniel. It was a side Seth preferred not to see.

The cart lurched, signaling Daniel's return to his place beside Simon. Seth opened his eyes. The Witchfinder and his men mounted their horses and spurred them into a gallop.

Seth twitched the reins and his horses started forward. He kept his gaze on the road.

"So, the witch thought she could escape, eh?" Daniel stood in the back of the cart and leaned over to speak to Seth. "Nobody gets away once I've arrested them. It's one in the eye for old Demdike though." Daniel chuckled.

Seth pursed his lips. He was in no mood to listen to Daniel's gloating.

Daniel folded his arms over the back of the seat. "So where are we taking our prisoner?"

"To Tom Barnett's wife, Miriam. She nursed her father for many years. She will know what to do."

"Miriam Barnett? That bad-tempered harridan?" Daniel laughed. "He may prefer the pillory to her ministrations."

"She is not the best choice." Seth spoke through gritted teeth.

"So why choose her?"

Seth pulled back on the reins. The cart stopped. Seth turned to face Daniel.

"Simon needs a healer. There is only one hereabouts with the skill to heal him, and we cannot go there."

Daniel stood upright, one hand on the seat. "Why not?"

"Because you have just sent her to her death." Seth whipped the reins. The cart jolted forward. Daniel pitched backwards. A grim smile formed on Seth's face at the sound of Daniel hitting the bare boards of the cart.

Chapter Twenty

Jessica woke to find Phenex seated at the end of her bed. He smiled and stood, displaying his attire. He wore a night-dress, a miniature copy of Jessica's own. She rolled her eyes and sat up.

"I saw you, last night, in the garden." She tried to imagine this boy as a fiery bird, but could not. The power he hid must be enormous.

"I've finished my part. The house and garden, and the trap below, are ready now."

"What of Demdike? Do you know?"

Phenex lost his smile. "Demdike is a danger to us. If Baal learns of our actions, he may transform Demdike into a Raven of Death. That would be bad enough. Worse, if the Golab is directly attacked by either us or Demdike, then Asmodeus will bring war to the world. We cannot kill the Witchfinder, nor can we allow Demdike to do it. The Golab's host body must perish by human hand, or within the trap we have set." He looked away. "The outcome is less certain now." Phenex walked to the door. "The others are gathered downstairs. Come down, when you are ready." He opened the door and left, closing it behind him.

Jessica hugged her knees. Foras's plan had seemed so easy, so straightforward. Now even the demons were worried. She threw back the blankets, dressed and went downstairs.

The hallway was empty. Jessica made her way to the kitchen, and found it stocked with fruit and vegetables. No meat. Belson sat on the table, his tail curled around his paws, and glared at the food available.

"Nothing here to your liking, Belson? I suppose our guests can't very well kill animals if they hope for redemption. I wonder if they eat at all." Jessica led Belson to the front door and opened it for him. She blinked in the sunshine and took a deep breath of the morning air.

Belson disappeared into the long grass opposite the house, no doubt in search of a fat mouse or dozing sparrow. Jessica closed the door and returned to the kitchen.

She breakfasted on an apple and a pear, then a handful of

plums, and went to search for the demons.

In the hallway, Jessica heard voices coming from the lounge, on the left side of the front door. She moved toward it, paused and stared at the door.

The two rabbits Simon left her were still hanging outside. Unless the rats and crows had seen through her spell, they should still be there. Jessica smiled as she opened the front door. Rabbit would be a treat for her supper, whether Foras approved or not.

She moved her hand over the space below the iron hook, muttering an incantation as she did so. The two rabbits reappeared, untouched by crows or ravens, although a little dry from their time in the sun.

"See, she makes rabbits appear from the air. The witch is revealed to us."

Jessica jumped at the sound of this shrill voice and tried to turn, but strong hands held her from behind.

A short man, dressed in Puritan black with white shirt and frilled collar, strolled into her line of sight. He smiled through his dark brown moustache and goatee as he raised his tall black hat, swinging his cane with his other hand.

"Mistress Chadwick, I presume?"

"Yes. Who are you?" Jessica saw nothing of the man who held her, but his grip was firm. Along the road, a third man sat on a horse and held the reins of two more.

Jessica glared at the short man and jutted her chin. "I have powerful friends, you know. Let me go." She squirmed as her hands were pulled behind her back and secured with coarse rope.

"Oh, I have no doubt your friends rank among the most powerful in Hell." The man's smile remained unmoved as he prodded her with his cane. "They will avail you nothing now. Allow me to introduce myself. I am Matthew Hopkins, and you, Jessica Chadwick, are a witch."

Jessica's mind raced. Here she stood, face to face with the Golab, while Foras and the other demons chatted inside the house. Phenex had told her the trap was ready. All she had to do was lead this creature inside.

"I'm no witch. Come visit with me a while, inside my cottage. You will see."

"We saw your illusion with our own eyes, witch." Hopkins leveled his cane at the two rabbits hanging outside the door. Fur fell in clumps as the flesh withered, dripping as a putrid liquid to pool on the ground beneath. Within moments, all that remained of the rabbits were two gore-flecked skeletons. Hopkins laughed.

"See how her magic fails in the face of righteous men. She cannot harm us now. We will take her to the mill pond we passed, beside the village, and test her there."

Swinging his cane over his shoulder, Hopkins walked away from the cottage. Jessica was lifted and slung over the strong man's shoulder, forced to breathe his sweat as he carried her away from her home, away from her only hope. She dared not call out to the demons. The Golab must remain unaware of them until he was within the house.

A dark shape detached itself from a clump of grass and moved toward the open door. Belson looked up at her, then dashed into the house. Jessica could have cried with relief. Foras would save her, or he would send one of the others to do it. Wouldn't he? He had told her of the restrictions on their actions here, how they could not interfere.

Jessica closed her eyes. She knew Bifrons, at least, was willing to bend the rules governing the demons' intervention in human lives. The last time he and Seere had saved her, she was alone in Demdike's tower. This time there would be witnesses. Foras might restrain Bifrons, since if the demons were revealed to the Golab it would become wary, and might escape the trap.

The man carrying Jessica threw her across the back of a horse. The impact drove the breath from her lungs, so she was unable to struggle when her feet were tied. Jessica stared into the grinning face of the Witchfinder for a moment, before he mounted his own horse.

Foras had mentioned the possibility of war if the Golab's master learned of their scheme. Jessica tried to think what she would do in his place. Without her, the trap had no bait, but if the Golab knew of the demons, the trap would fail anyway. If the demons interfered directly with the Golab, then Asmodeus might be invoked. Jessica gritted her teeth. Somehow she had to get away from the Golab, because Foras could not help her in his presence.

Chapter Twenty-One

The first thing Simon saw when he opened his eyes was the severe expression on Miriam Barnett's face. Her hair was hidden beneath her white cloth cap, but the steel gray of her eyes held him like the gaze of a snake.

"He's awake." She sat up and busied herself with something at her side. Tom Barnett's face came into view.

"Simon? How are you?"

Simon grunted and tried to sit up. He wanted to ask how long he had slept, but his voice failed him. Miriam's strong hand pressed him back down.

"Stay there. Leave him alone, Tom. He needs rest." She lifted a wet cloth and pressed it to his face. Simon gasped at the heat in the cloth and moved his head away. Miriam held his head with one hand and pressed the cloth to his cheek with the other.

"Stop wriggling or I'll have to tie you down. This will take away some of the swelling."

Simon closed his eyes against the pain in his face, now compounded by the trickles of hot water that ran along the side of his head. His last memory was of the barn, of fighting to stay awake so he could talk to Daniel when he arrived. Now he was in the care of Miriam and Tom Barnett, no longer in the barn and clearly not in the pillory. Rather, he lay on a soft bed in, he assumed, Tom's house.

Something must have happened to Daniel, something must have distracted him from Simon's punishment. There was only one thing Daniel would regard as more important than pinning Simon back into the pillory. The possibility of a hanging.

"Jessica." Simon breathed the name. His eyes opened. Miriam's hand tensed against his cheek.

"Don't you concern yourself with her." Miriam took the cloth from his face and dipped it into the steaming bowl at her side. "We all saw what she tried to do in the square. You were lucky Seth and Daniel arrived when they did."

The laugh forming in Simon's throat changed into a fit of coughing. It had been a long time since he considered any meeting with Daniel to be lucky. He sat up, with Miriam's help, until the cough subsided. Miriam held a cup of cool water to his lips. Simon tried to gulp it, but Miriam allowed him only a few sips. She took the cup away. Only then did Simon realize that he was naked and covered only with a thick woolen blanket. He tried to grasp the blanket and pull it to himself, but his fingers had no strength. He could barely bend them without pain.

"Where are my clothes?"

"Your clothes are filthy." Miriam dropped the cloth into the hot water and pushed him back onto the bed with both hands. "Did you think I would let you in my house with that stink? I have put your clothes to soak in the basin outside. You can use some of Tom's old clothes until they've dried."

She gave a tight smile as she pulled the blanket up to his chin. "Don't worry, it was Tom and Seth who undressed you and washed you while you slept. I have enough to put up with as it is, with Daniel Featherstone and his vile pipe smoking up my house."

"Dan is here? I have to speak to him."

"You have to rest. I'm going to get you some rabbit stew." Miriam stood and placed the bowl on the cabinet beside the bed. "It is leftovers, but it'll be fine when I've warmed it up." She paused at the door. "I made it from the rabbits you sold us a few days ago, so it's best you finish it before you speak to the bailiff." She closed the door. Simon listened to her footsteps receding down the stairs. He raised his head to look around the room.

It was more like a store room than a bedroom. Spools of colored yarn filled the spaces between the few sticks of furniture and carefully folded lengths of cloth were piled high on a chair and a small table against the far wall. Beside the bed were the chair Miriam had sat on and the cabinet that now held the bowl of hot water. Behind Simon, sunlight showed through an open window, and the faint chatter of the villagers outside blended into an indecipherable murmur.

Simon sat up again. Against the pain, fatigue and nausea, he swung his legs over the side of the bed. The door creaked as it opened. Simon looked up.

"I see you have ignored Miriam's instructions." Seth Crocker's bulk filled the doorway. "I suspected you would. Here, Tom has provided clothes for you." Seth walked to where Simon swayed on the bed and placed a bundle of clothes beside him. "Can you dress yourself?"

"I don't know." Simon examined his hands. They tingled with

returning sensation, but there was no strength in his fingers and it hurt to move them. "I can try."

Seth pulled a pair of gray trousers from the bundle and knelt to slip them over Simon's feet. Simon tried to help, but Seth brushed his hands away.

"Save your strength. You will need it to endure Miriam's cooking."

"Why are you helping me, Seth? Yesterday you helped Dan take Jessica away. What has changed you?"

Seth lifted Simon from the bed to finish pulling up the trousers, then sat him gently back down.

"Changed me? What do you mean?" He lifted a white shirt and held it so that Simon could insert his arms. "She wanted to harm you. She made blue fire in the air. We all saw it."

"When have you ever known Jessica Chadwick harm anyone?" Simon's fingers fumbled at the buttons of the shirt. Seth took over once more.

"Truth be told, I have never heard of the woman doing anything but good. That's why I was pleased to hear she had escaped Demdike."

Simon's head shot up, too fast. Spots blurred his vision. His head swam. "She escaped?"

Seth finished with the buttons and took a step back. "Much good it will do her. That Matthew Hopkins, who calls himself Witchfinder-General, is here."

Simon drew a long, slow breath. The cool air caught in his throat and set him coughing again. Seth leaned forward and slapped Simon's back until the cough subsided.

"Well, you look better, and I must say you smell a lot better." Seth said. "So, if she wasn't trying to kill you, what was Miss Chadwick doing?"

"Trying to help me. I don't know what she intended but I'm sure of it. Either to heal me, or release me from the pillory."

"I don't know." Seth scratched his head. "That fire she made looked dangerous."

"Jessica would never harm me." Simon pushed against the bed, but his legs would not bear his weight. He sat back, defeated. "I have to help her. If she is free of Demdike, I have to get her away from here before the Witchfinder catches her."

Seth settled onto the chair Miriam had vacated. "Why, Simon? You will end up hanging alongside her. Let justice take its course. If she is innocent, she will be freed."

"Seth, you are too trusting. This Witchfinder cares nothing for guilt or innocence. He is paid for convictions, not acquittals."

"I see the truth of your words, Simon, but what are we to do about it? She performed magic at the Mayday fair, for all to see. I have heard people blame her for the dead animals. Miriam believes she is guilty of dabbling in the black arts, though Tom is not convinced."

Seth turned his face to the window. "Dan is sure of her guilt, I think, but he might just want a hanging. He has changed, I think, but I cannot seem to remember how he was before."

"That's because of Demdike." Simon pressed the palm of his hand to his jaw. All this talking had started an ache. "He killed the animals. I saw what he did to some Roundhead soldiers. He skinned them alive, and cut out their tongues. Demdike has stolen our thoughts, all of us."

Seth's face wrinkled in disgust. "Demdike is unpleasant, but it is hard to imagine him capable of such things. He is a very old man. You really think he could overpower a group of soldiers?" Seth leaned forward in his chair. "Are you sure you didn't dream all this, when you were chained in the barn?"

"It's no dream. Demdike is the true evil in this village. He wants Jessica, but I'm not sure why. He thinks the Witchfinder will help him."

"I doubt it." Seth raised his eyebrows. "If you had heard the names that man called Demdike this morning, even you would blush."

"Get Dan." Simon tried to rise again. His knees buckled. Seth grabbed him before he could fall and sat him back on the bed. Simon took several deep breaths and held his mouth still to quell the surge of pain that shot through his cheek. "Get Dan up here. I can prove Demdike has bewitched us."

"What are you doing?" Miriam stood in the doorway holding a bowl, from which steam curled upwards. The smell of overcooked rabbit stew filled the room. "Why is he already dressed?" She stomped to the bed, placed the stew next to the bowl of hot water and pushed Seth toward the door. "Out, out until he has eaten."

In other circumstances, Simon might have laughed aloud at the look on Seth's face as a woman half his size propelled him from the room. Today his thoughts were concerned with how he would prove to Daniel and Seth that their memories had been changed by Demdike's spells. He nodded to himself. If their false memories were the same as his, there was one thing that must surely convince them. Simon sat as upright as he could manage while Miriam collected the bowl of stew and took the seat Seth had just vacated.

"Well, since you're sitting up anyway, you can feed yourself." Miriam's eyes glittered as she held the bowl out to Simon. A spoon lay in the stew, its handle toward him. Simon reached out to grasp the spoon.

His knuckles refused to bend at first, and then his fingers curled slowly around the handle. Simon raised his hand, but the spoon slid from between his fingers and splashed into the hot stew.

"I thought as much." Miriam's lips thinned into a tight smile. "My father was the same way. Always insisting he was well enough to do things for himself." She picked the spoon from the bowl. "Now you just be quiet and let me feed you."

"What am I to do with no hands?" Simon stared at his curled fingers. "I can't set a snare with these."

"They'll heal. Too long in the pillory and manacles, but they'll heal. You just have to rest them for a day or two. Now stop feeling sorry for yourself and eat. This stew won't stay hot forever." Miriam lifted the spoon to Simon's lips.

The hot liquid seared into the cuts in Simon's mouth, and drilled into the spaces where his teeth had been knocked out. He jerked his head back. Stew spilled from the spoon onto his chest.

"Oh, now you've ruined a good shirt." Miriam gave an exasperated sigh. "Well, there's no sense in changing it until you've finished." She lifted the spoon again.

Simon sipped with more caution this time. He managed to swallow a little of the stew. Its warmth spread into his body, and reawakened his hunger. Soon, the bowl was empty and most of the stew was inside Simon, although the front of his borrowed shirt was streaked with spillage. Simon probed the new gaps in his teeth with his tongue. They still hurt, but the pain had reduced.

"Is he finished?" Seth stood in the doorway.

"Yes, but he should rest now." Miriam stood, wiping at her apron. Some of Simon's stew had stained more than his shirt. "I'll have to find him another shirt, since you were in such a hurry to get him into that one." She shot a glare at Seth.

"I am sorry, Miriam. I did not like to see him so dependant. It is not Simon's way to ask for favors. You know that."

"Favors." Miriam bustled to the door. "If helping a friend in need counts as a favor now, then the world has moved a step closer to Hell." She brushed Seth aside. Behind him stood Daniel, his thumbs hooked into his waistcoat. Miriam stopped and stared at Daniel.

"Have you come to see the result of your work, Daniel Featherstone? He is lucky to be alive, no thanks to you." Miriam's jaw jutted.

"It was Lord West who sentenced him to the pillory. I was just doing my job." Daniel avoided Miriam's gaze.

"Miriam, please, let them in." Simon spoke between long breaths, afraid to move too fast in case his stomach rejected his food. "I have to speak to them. Both of them."

Miriam looked from one to the other. "Five minutes," she said. "No more. I will send Tom up to make sure you two leave." She glared at Simon. "Then I expect you to sleep." Miriam pushed past Daniel. Nobody moved or spoke until her footsteps reached the bottom of the stairs.

Daniel's discomfort showed through his chuckle. "This or the pillory, Simon. Not much of a choice, eh?"

"An easy choice, Dan." Simon shifted along the bed until he could rest his back against the headboard. "Miriam may be harsh, but she is a good woman at heart. You have no heart at all."

"Brave words, from a criminal." Daniel moved forward.

Seth put himself between Daniel and Simon. "You two can fight another time. Simon, what is it you wanted to prove to us?" Seth pulled the chair away from the bed and motioned Daniel to sit. Seth sat at the end of Simon's bed.

Simon took a deep breath. "Demdike is the one you want, Dan. His witchcraft is the cause of all our troubles. Don't you remember what it was like before he came here?"

Daniel blinked. "He was here before I was born. How can I remember anything before that?"

"No, he wasn't." Simon sighed. "Try to remember, both of you. Remember when you were children? Remember the games we used to play at the tower?"

"Yes, we used to dare each other to touch that black tower." Seth nodded. "We all played it. I remember..." Seth's eyes narrowed. He shook his head. "That can't be right."

"You're seeing through it, Seth. Demdike took little care with his spell. He thought us all simple country folk, easily duped. He made mistakes in the memories he planted." Simon shifted his weight to reduce the ache in his back.

"What's all this?" Daniel sat back in the chair and crossed his legs. "Believe me, I would dearly love to have Demdike at the end of a rope, but the two of you are speaking in riddles. What do childhood games have to do with anything?"

Simon forced his fingers to flex. Miriam had said they would heal in a few days, but he had no time to waste. "Think, Dan. Who played those games?"

Daniel shrugged. "The three of us, and Tom, and—"

"The three of us. Children together." Simon leaned forward. "I'm forty-six years old, Dan. You are close to my age. Tom is a few years older." Simon turned to Seth, whose mouth gaped below wide eyes. "Seth here—"

"I am twenty-eight." Seth spoke in a flat tone. "So you two would have been..." He ducked his head to count on his fingers.

"I was eighteen when you were born." Simon watched Daniel's face as he spoke. "So were you, Dan. We did not play together as children. We never dared each other to touch Demdike's tower. Nobody did, because the tower wasn't there."

"Wasn't there?" Daniel's eyes glazed. "That can't be right."

"It's true, Dan. I remember." Seth stared at his hands. "I remember many things now. I have driven my cart on Lord West's land for many years. The tower is recent." Seth screwed up his face. "I don't remember any building work though. One day there was no tower, the next day it was there, complete, with Demdike in it."

"It arrived in the night." Simon looked from Daniel to Seth. Both appeared dazed. He hoped their minds could cope with what was happening. Simon needed Seth, at least, to carry him. Daniel's authority would be of use if they had to confront the Witchfinder.

"Arrived?" A weak smile showed on Daniel's face. "Buildings don't just arrive. Someone has to build them."

Simon slapped the backs of his hands against his thighs. "It arrived, Dan. A demon brought it. Demdike is in league with demons."

"Like the Chadwick woman? Demdike is one of her group?" Daniel's eyes narrowed.

"No, Dan. Jessica is innocent. She has some skills but she has only ever used them to heal people. Jessica does not consort with demons." Simon thought of Orobas, the demon Jessica had named at the fair, but thought it best to keep that knowledge to himself for now.

"So Demdike is another witch." Daniel stood up. "The Witchfinder is here. He must be told of this."

Simon placed his palms to his forehead. Daniel refused to see the truth, and took refuge in his duties. There must be a way to convince him. Seth placed his hand on Simon's arm.

"Dan is right. We have to tell the Witchfinder about Demdike." He gave Simon a look filled with hidden meaning.

Simon nodded. At least Seth had accepted the truth. Even if Daniel refused to believe his memories were all lies, he would still denounce Demdike to the Witchfinder. That might distract attention from Jessica long enough to let her escape. Simon decided to let things stand for now. If he put too much pressure on Daniel, he would only enrage the man and might even end up back in the pillory.

"So where is the Witchfinder now?" Simon asked.

Seth looked at Daniel, who raised his eyebrows in response.

"He is searching for the escaped witch." Daniel inspected his fingernails.

"Dan sent him to Jessica's home." Seth spoke to Simon. "If she has any sense she will not be there. After her escape, she must surely realize these people will not welcome her back."

Simon narrowed his eyes at Daniel. He wished he had full use of his hands, and something sharp to fill them, but there was no use in wishing.

The murmur from outside the window grew in intensity. Someone shouted. Simon strained to hear. Seth and Daniel went to the window.

"What's happening?" Simon pulled himself up on shaky legs. He stumbled against the cabinet and knocked the bowl of water to the floor.

"Can't tell yet." Seth caught Simon's arm and supported him as he approached the window. "There's someone climbing up on the pillory platform."

Warm water soaked the soles of Simon's bare feet. He ignored this minor discomfort as he squinted through the window. The three of them leaned out as far as they dared.

Along the street, the village square was visible, and part of the pillory platform. Simon could not see who was speaking, but he caught the words 'mill pond' from the excited speaker. People began running along the street, from the square.

They called to others as they passed beneath the window. Most of what they said was lost in the general noise, but the words Simon could make out chilled his blood.

They've caught the witch!

Chapter Twenty-Two

The villagers gathered at the river, beside the deep pool of the mill house. Jessica watched them arrive, saw the excitement in their eyes, heard the anticipation in their babbling voices. She knelt on the damp soil, her hands still tied. Jessica bowed her head, trying to shut out the bloodlust emanating from the approaching crowd.

There were none among them she could call a close friend, but none she would consider an enemy. Yet they acted as though she had committed some terrible crime, as though they had known all along she was wicked and deserved punishment.

Jessica fought back tears. They would not break her with their vindictive thoughts. While she lived, there was a chance her demons would save her. First, though, she would have to escape on her own. With all these people here, and with the Witchfinder so close, Foras would never permit the demons to intervene.

The Witchfinder's accomplices stood to either side, so she dare not speak any magic. Their auras were bright with the blue of men who truly believed that what they did was right, but streaks of sickly yellow showed her the deceptions they were under. They had been infected with Hopkins' evil, though they did not recognize the influence it had on them.

Jessica looked again at the Witchfinder, who now stood with his back to her, his arms extended in welcome to the crowd. She half-closed her eyes, but could still make out no aura around him. To her normal sight, he was a small and unimposing man. To her witch-sight, it was as if he was not there at all. The Golab gave nothing away. The only clue to its presence was, it seemed, the absence of anything at all. Jessica wondered if the soul of Matthew Hopkins still lived within his body, or whether the Golab had consumed him when it took possession. The Witchfinder turned and pointed at her.

"Jessica Chadwick, you are accused of witchcraft. Namely that you did bewitch and mutilate livestock belonging to these good people, that you have conversed with devils and demons, consorted with the vile spawn of the Ungodly, and made spells and potions intending to harm your neighbors." Hopkins hauled her to her feet. "Confess before these people, before your God, and you may yet be spared."

"I have done none of these things." Jessica spoke with confidence, despite knowing that she was guilty, at least, of conversation with demons. Jessica's house was currently overrun with fallen angels. She allowed herself a tight smile as she imagined how these people might react if they knew.

The Witchfinder leaned in close and whispered. "You do not fear me enough. I taste so little from you. You will give me more before we are done. There is power in you and I will have its strength." He stood and spoke aloud. "Lies. The false tongue of the witch drips with venom and guile. The water will bring the truth from her."

Hopkins pushed her toward the two men, who caught her and spun her to lie face down on the ground. The men untied her hands before flipping her onto her back. They held her down. Jessica turned her head to one side and stared along the riverbank.

Some distance away, enormous spider legs poked from between the reeds. The ruddy face of Bifrons appeared, his needle teeth bared in a grin. He waved briefly, before a large hand appeared above his head, grabbed him and pulled him back. Behind Bifrons, something slipped into the water.

Jessica struggled to breathe under the weight on her chest. One of the men pulled her right foot up to her waist, while the other held her left arm. Hopkins tied her left thumb to her right big toe with twine.

They repeated the process with her left big toe and right thumb before the men released their hold on her. Jessica screamed as the truth of the rumors she'd heard manifested in the pain of her bonds.

Hopkins stood back. The two men lifted her and held her over the deep mill pool. Hopkins tied a long rope around her waist.

"You can't do this. I am innocent." Jessica fought the bonds, but movement simply made them cut deeper.

"Test the witch." The voice came from the crowd, soon joined by others.

"She killed my sheep. Tore out their eyes and tongues."

"Took the hearts from my best cattle."

"Gave my son the fever."

Hysteria rose like a wave to drown the common sense of the people. Jessica twisted to see Hopkins, his grin displaying his enjoyment of the proceedings. These people knew her, she had healed many of them, cured ailments, headaches, diseases, aches. She had set bones for them, stitched wounds, used herbs and invocations to speed healing. She had harmed none. They must know this, but the frenzy of the witch hunt was on them now.

"Let the water be our judge." Hopkins released the coil of rope in his hand but kept hold of the end. He nodded. The two men swung Jessica and hurled her into the pond.

The water shocked the breath from her lungs. Its cold surged into her mouth, cut across her eyes, numbed her skin. Jessica struggled to reach the surface but the manner of her bondage made any attempt at swimming impossible. The thought of failure burned her mind, hiding any fear for her own death.

Warmth enveloped her, arms folded around her. Above, sunlight flickered on the ripples of the river. A mouth closed over hers, breathing air into her lungs. Jessica opened her eyes as her savior drew back. He was handsome, with ice-blue eyes and curled blonde hair.

"I am Crocell," he said. "I am here to save you."

Light bloomed as they rose to the surface. Crocell held her from beneath, letting her head break the surface. Jessica spat water from her mouth and looked into the furious eyes of the Witchfinder as she drifted toward the bank, pulled by the Witchfinder's rope.

"She floats." Hopkins spoke through a sneer.

Jessica narrowed her eyes. Hopkins must have expected her to sink so he could have applied further tests. She knew what those tests entailed. He and his men would take turns to keep her awake for days. They'd prick her with a sliding blade so they would appear to stab her without drawing blood. There would be a search for the devil's mark, a mole or a birthmark or an old scar. They would search for a familiar, such as a toad or a black cat, in her house. Belson, if they found him, would be all the evidence they would need.

The Golab would have feasted on her fear over the coming days if she had not been proven a witch by their swimming test. Jessica was happy to disappoint him.

One of Hopkins' men pulled her from the water and dropped her, gasping, onto the bank. The demons had saved her from drowning, and from subsequent torture, but they had hastened her condemnation.

"See, the water rejects her." Hopkins spoke to the crowd. "She is a witch, delivered into our hands by the Almighty."

The twine binding her thumbs and toes was cut. Hopkins' men hauled her to her feet and held her upright. Jessica's wet clothes stuck to her skin. She shivered with cold.

"Prepare a gallows. We will send this witch to Hell." The crowd roared as Hopkins, his arms spread wide, incited them to higher and higher insanity.

"Stop."

Silence fell, and the crowd turned to this new voice. Hopkins dropped his arms to his sides, his face darkening.

Lord West sat on his noble brown horse. Beside him rode three of his retainers, one of whom led a riderless steed. Behind them, cowled as always, Demdike sat astride a gaunt and wild-eyed black horse. Jessica felt for the poor beast, forced to carry such a loathsome burden.

"Release the woman." Lord West's imperious tone made the crowd back away. "This is no trial. It is a travesty. You, Witchfinder, are a fraud. I will take this woman and investigate the claims against her."

As Lord West spoke, Demdike urged his horse forward until he was beside the lord.

Two of the lord's men dismounted and moved toward Jessica. The two men holding Jessica tightened their grip. The lord's men halted with uncertainty in their eyes.

"I said, release her." Lord West produced a flintlock and aimed it at Hopkins, who curled his lip but nodded to his men.

Jessica fell forward, to be caught by the lord's men. They half-carried, half-dragged her to the waiting horse and helped her into the saddle. She caught sight of Demdike's grin beneath his hood, and wondered whether hanging might be preferable to whatever this monster had in mind.

Hopkins stepped forward. He pointed his shaking finger at Lord West. "You are interfering in God's work. The Almighty will have his revenge, and I will have my witch."

Hopkins transferred his attention to Demdike. "This vile creature has corrupted you all. It is at his behest that this witch escapes justice." He lowered his voice to address Demdike directly. "I know what you are. This woman's death is mine. I claim her."

The smile fell from Demdike's mouth. His lips moved, but no sound came out. Jessica wondered at this silent incantation, and at the abrupt silence that came over the crowd of villagers.

"Leave this place, Witchfinder, and never set foot on my lands again." The imperious tone in Lord West's voice brooked no argument. Jessica held the horn of the saddle as her horse was led away. Behind her, the murmur of the crowd returned, drowned for a moment by a howl of pure rage. She had no need to turn to know the source. The Golab blasted its fury through the mouth of a man. The Witchfinder roared, but the Golab howled within him.

Chapter Twenty-Three

Seth sat at the front of his cart and picked up the reins. "You sure you're not coming with us, Tom?"

Tom pursed his lips and glanced at his front door. "No, I'd best stay with Miriam. She's right about Simon, you know. You should leave him here."

"I have to go. Everybody thinks Jessica tried to kill me. They won't believe it from Seth and Dan. I have to tell them myself." Simon sat in the back of the cart, where Seth had placed him after helping him down the stairs. "Tell Miriam I'm sorry to leave like this. I know she doesn't approve." Simon lowered his voice to a whisper. "I'll bring you a couple of rabbits when I'm back at work."

Tom smiled. "You take your time, Simon." He moved closer to the cart to avoid Miriam's hearing. "She'll just burn them anyway."

"There's no time for idle chit-chat." Daniel had moved to the far side of the cart and now climbed up to sit beside Seth. "Let's get moving. I'm looking forward to handing Demdike's name to this Witchfinder." He rubbed his hands and grinned. "Maybe there's a reward in it."

With a last nod to Tom, Seth flicked the reins and the cart moved forward.

The cart rolled out of the village. Seth turned it toward the mill. His horses kept a steady pace over the old track, but the mill road was notorious for potholes. More than once Seth had to slow the cart to negotiate a particularly rough patch.

"Can't this thing go any faster?" Daniel almost bounced in his seat in his impatience. "Come on, Seth, give these nags a taste of the lash."

Seth bit his lip. "My horses have never been lashed."

"Well, if they were, you might get a bit more out of them."

"Look at the road, Dan. If we go too fast, this old cart will throw a wheel or fall apart. I'm going as fast as I dare." Seth kept his eyes ahead, watching for holes in the road.

Daniel folded his arms. "I could walk faster."

Seth clenched his teeth. He knew Daniel was unlikely to walk if there was a ride to be had. If not for Simon and the urgency of their trip, Seth would have slowed the cart to a crawl to infuriate the fat bailiff. He checked the road ahead, then risked a glance at Simon.

"You all right back there, Simon?"

"Don't worry about me. I'll be fine," Simon said. "There's a quicker way to the mill though, across the fields."

Seth shook his head. "Sure there is. Only, you can barely walk and my cart can't hop fences or streams. It takes a few minutes longer this way, but we'll get there."

The cart lurched over a series of small holes. Seth returned his attention to the road and kept it there. They were less than half a mile from the mill house. He had only to keep his cart moving for another five minutes or so.

Seth had delivered grain to the mill many times, and taken away sacks of flour. He knew this road well enough to realize complacency could be the undoing of any cart here. Some holes were constant, but new ones appeared all the time, especially after rain.

It had been years since Lord West had last ordered the potholes filled. Seth narrowed his eyes. There had been little maintenance on the estate in recent years. Lord West had once been a good landowner but he had become withdrawn and uncaring since Demdike's appearance. Seth gripped the reins tighter. The sooner this village was rid of Demdike, the better.

Ahead, the rutted track joined with the road that led to Lord West's mansion. The junction was obscured by trees, so Seth slowed his horses to be ready to stop.

Daniel hissed through his teeth. "Why are we slowing down again? We'll never get there at this rate."

"I can't see around corners, Dan. Don't fret, we're only a couple of minutes from the millhouse."

A howl tore the air. Seth's horses reared, and he pulled at their reins to steady them. Daniel grabbed the seat with his hands. Simon pulled himself up to look over the front of the cart. Seth found he had stopped breathing, and forced his chest to move. His horses whinnied, but stood still. The world darkened although the sky was almost cloudless. The birds fell silent.

The howl died away. Seth noticed his hands shaking and pressed them to his knees. Daniel's face was deathly white. Seth turned to Simon, who stared ahead with wide eyes. The birds resumed their song, sunlight returned to the world. Seth shuddered. He felt as though Death itself had brushed them in its passing.

Daniel found his voice first. "What was that?" His words,

barely a whisper, echoed among the resonances of the howl that still occupied Seth's skull.

"Jessica." Simon breathed the name.

"No." Seth squared his jaw. "That was no woman's scream." Seth took a deep breath. "Whatever that was, it was no human, or indeed animal sound that I have ever heard before." He pressed his horses forward.

"Perhaps we should report to Lord West first." Daniel's voice trembled. "Before we accuse Demdike to the Witchfinder."

"Don't let him sway you, Seth. That sound came from the mill. We have to see what it was." Simon hooked his elbows over the back of Seth's seat.

"Well, it will take no time to do what Dan wants." Seth nodded at the road ahead. "Here comes Lord West now, and Demdike is with him." Seth turned back to Simon. "You shouldn't be here. Best get under that tarpaulin and lay still. If his Lordship sees you, we'll all have questions to answer."

"That's right." Daniel turned in his seat and leaned over to pull the tarpaulin over Simon, who lay down on the boards. "I'll get the worst of it. I'm supposed to have you in the pillory, not riding around the countryside. You stay silent."

Seth checked that the bunched-up tarpaulin did not easily reveal the body beneath, then pulled the cart to the side of the road to let Lord West's group pass.

His Lordship ignored them, but Demdike bared yellow teeth at Daniel as he passed. Seth raised an eyebrow when he saw Jessica being led by one of Lord West's men and flanked by two more.

Daniel started to speak, but Seth jabbed his elbow into Daniel's ribs to silence him. Mention of Jessica's name might draw Simon from his hiding place.

Jessica held her head high. She glared at them both, her lip curled in a sneer, but she said nothing.

Seth waited until the riders had passed out of sight. A smile creased his lips.

"I didn't hear you speak to Lord West, Dan. I thought you wanted to condemn Demdike."

Daniel looked away. "Yes, but not while the old devil is present. If half of what Simon says is true, that would be unwise."

"Unwise indeed. Some might say fatal." With the grim smile still on his face, Seth set his horses moving. The mill lay just around a bend in the road, and it sounded like there was a commotion building there.

Dan sighed. He leaned back in the seat. "You can get up now, Simon. They've gone."

Simon struggled from beneath the heavy tarpaulin. "What was that about? Why was Demdike here?"

"It seems he has rescued your witch friend from the Witchfinder." Daniel ran his tongue over his teeth. "A temporary reprieve, once the Witchfinder knows Demdike is another of her kind."

"She is not like him." Simon sat up. "Dan, try to understand. Demdike is evil. Jessica is not."

"A witch is a witch." Daniel said.

"There's your Witchfinder." Seth pulled the cart to a stop a few yards from the crowd at the river. He was grateful for the opportunity to interrupt Dan and Simon. They were unlikely to reach any kind of agreement, and if it came to blows Seth would have to choose a side. His mind floundered with new knowledge, and he still had to come to terms with the realization that many of his memories were lies. It was a bad time to make decisions.

Daniel climbed from the cart, puffed out his chest and pushed through the crowd. Seth had a view over the crowd from his seat on the cart, and wondered if the Witchfinder would be receptive to Daniel's accusations. The small man looked as furious as he had that morning, at Demdike's door. One of the Witchfinder's men led three horses along the riverbank, toward the crowd.

Nobody paid the slightest attention to Seth's cart. The villagers ignored Daniel as he pushed through them. Their attention seemed focused on the Witchfinder. It was as though they waited for something. Seth frowned. He saw nothing to explain the howl they had heard, but something seemed wrong.

Simon leaned over the seat. "What's going on, Seth? What's wrong with them all?"

"So you've noticed it too."

"I've never seen the like. It's as if they've been frozen." Simon lost his grip on the seat and fell backwards. He regained his position with a mixture of grunts and curses.

Daniel reached the Witchfinder and was speaking. The Witchfinder shrugged at his words. Evidently he had no interest in Daniel's condemnation of Demdike. The Witchfinder took the reins of his horse. His men climbed into their saddles. The villagers moved forward.

Daniel and the Witchfinder faced the crowd. His men backed their horses away, but the crowd ignored them. They seemed intent on Daniel and the Witchfinder.

"I don't like this. These people are acting like a pack of wolves." Seth spoke in a low voice.

"Is it something to do with that howling we heard?" Simon settled his elbows over the back of the seat. "Something Demdike did to them?"

"That howl wasn't a wolf. It wasn't like any animal I ever heard." Seth rose from his seat. "I'm going to find out what's happening. You'd best stay here for now." He jumped to the ground just as Daniel raised his arms to address the crowd.

"Listen to me. Demdike is a witch. He has saved one of his own from justice. We have to capture them both." Daniel shouted over the rising grumble of the crowd. "Listen to me. I am the bailiff for this land, and I say Jessica Chadwick and Nicholas Demdike must be brought to justice."

The crowd snarled. Seth stopped at the rear of the crowd. It was definitely a snarl he had heard, issuing from all their mouths in unison. He reached for the nearest person, put his hand on the man's shoulder and turned him around.

Seth released the man's shoulder the moment he saw his face. It was Robert Davies. His lips were drawn back over his teeth, his eyes blazed with fury. Seth struggled for words. He had never seen Robert like this. The carpenter was one of the most easygoing men he knew, but now he looked ready to tear flesh with his teeth.

"Robert. What's wrong with you?" Seth took a step backwards.

"Fraud." Robert spat the word. "Lord West said so. The fraud wanted to kill Jessica Chadwick, but she has done nothing."

"Fraud." The crowd repeated in unison. "Tried to kill an innocent woman."

"Innocent?" Daniel's voice carried over the heads of the people. "She made blue fire in the square. She controlled a horse with a few words. You all saw it." There was a tremor in his voice.

"We saw nothing."

Seth held his breath. He heard the monks chant at prayer in Marchway, all singing the same words together. It impressed him, but hearing these people do the same, terrified him. It was unnatural, it was wrong. Robert turned back to the crowd. Seth held his ground, too scared to move forward, too fascinated to run.

"What is this? Yesterday you spurned the woman. You wanted to hang her. Today you defend her?" Daniel's voice became shrill.

"Fraud. Lies." The crowd rushed toward the river. Daniel

screamed. The Witchfinder's men spurred their horses and fled along the road.

The howl came again.

Seth clamped his hands over his ears. He turned, briefly, to see Simon with his arms over his head. The crowd surged like a wave, snarling and growling.

Something spurted among the people. A thin red fountain shot up in their midst. Seth's stomach constricted. The crowd shrieked its glee. They held aloft the sleeve of Daniel's jacket. Daniel's hand protruded from the cuff, still twitching. Seth fell to his knees and surrendered his breakfast to the grass.

A thud marked the arrival of Daniel's head at the edge of the crowd. Seth stared into those dead eyes, at that shocked expression, and retched again. His mind spun, centered on Simon's remark.

Something Demdike did to them.

Seth knew these people. He knew many of their children. They were good people, never prone to violence. This was not natural. Simon was right. Demdike must be killed, but how? If Daniel was torn apart, then the Witchfinder must also be dead. The village was under Demdike's control, as was Lord West. Only Simon and himself now knew the truth, and what could they do?

The crowd fell silent.

Seth stood up and wiped his eyes and mouth with his shirt.

A woman screamed. People staggered from the crowd. They stared at the blood spattered over their clothes and faces, their eyes wild. Seth watched them run to the road, the fields, the woods. They ran away, heedless of direction.

Some ten people now remained among the scattered remains of Daniel Featherstone. Seth took a deep breath and moved forward, even as the remaining people took a step back. Between them, Seth saw the Witchfinder. He lay on his back, his shoes were gone and his hands and feet were trussed together. Beside him lay the dismembered and disemboweled torso of Daniel.

"Don't let them kill him, Seth." Simon spoke from his place in the cart. "He's the only one who can help us against Demdike. Tell him we'll let him go if he leaves Jessica alone."

One of the men tied the long rope around the Witchfinder's waist. Seth stepped among the men. "What are you doing? Is one death not enough?"

"We have a mind to try him with his own test." Robert stood before Seth. "He is a fraud. Dan Featherstone also. Dan was guilty of helping this wicked man, and of pretending to find a witch." Robert spoke without inflection. His eyes showed none of their earlier fury, rather they resembled the blank stare Seth had seen moments before, on Daniel's dead face.

"Release me, you idiots." The Witchfinder shouted at the men who lifted him from the ground. "Release me and there will be no punishment. You have been bewitched. I can help you." He struggled as the men carried him to the mill pond. "Release me, I say, or the consequences will be terrible indeed." He turned his face to where Seth stood.

Matthew Hopkins' eyes opened wide. "You," he said. "The big man. You refused to help me this morning. Help me now." Hopkins' eyes darkened. The black of his pupils bled into their colored surround and spread until they covered the whites.

Behind Seth, Simon gasped. "Dear God, he's like Demdike."

Seth grasped Robert's shoulders. "These thoughts are not your own. Demdike has deceived us all. Stop this madness."

Robert ignored Seth's grip. He watched as the Witchfinder splashed into the river. The water closed over the bound form, then parted again. The Witchfinder rose to the surface.

"He floats." Robert spoke in a monotone. There was silence as the men pulled the Witchfinder back to the bank and hauled him from the water. Seth released Robert's shoulders and moved to untie the Witchfinder, but three men blocked his path.

"Seth." Simon shouted from the cart. "Seth, get us out of here."

Seth pushed one of the men aside, but another took his place.

"Seth, for God's sake look at him." Simon's voice became urgent. "Look. He's not even wet."

The Witchfinder's hair and clothes showed no evidence of his visit to the deep pool. Seth shook his head. The remnants of the crowd gathered around.

"The water rejects him." Robert showed no emotion. "He is a witch. Suffer ye not a witch to live."

Every Sunday, almost everyone in the village took the long walk to the church, halfway between here and Marchway. That was where Seth heard those words before. Many times, over the years, although this was the first time he had been confronted with the reality of their meaning.

"Robert, come to your senses. This is not the way." Seth spoke without conviction. The Witchfinder's eyes, and his repulsion of the water, made Seth wonder if this were indeed a man he was trying to save.

"Come on, Seth. Leave him to them. We have to save Jessica from Demdike," Simon called. Seth ignored him.

"You will pay dearly for this." The Witchfinder pulled at his bonds but could not free them. A trickle of blood showed where the twine cut into his thumbs. He rolled onto his side.

One of the men lifted a heavy stone from the riverbank and dropped it onto the Witchfinder's ribs. The cracking of bone was followed by the wheeze of damaged lungs. The others followed suit, each with the largest stone they could carry. They broke his arms and legs, crushed his ribs, and still he lived. Robert carried his stone to the Witchfinder's head. He lifted it high, then threw it down.

Seth closed his eyes to avoid the sight, but he could not close his ears to the crack of the skull, and the wet slap of its contents hitting the earth. He headed to his cart without looking back. Simon's ashen face told him all he needed to know.

The first shout came just as Seth placed his hand on the side of the cart. There was another, and another. Seth forced himself to face the blood-spattered scene.

From the Witchfinder's broken body, a black fog rose. Seth pressed his back to his cart. The fog produced tendrils that lanced toward each of the ten men. Even as the central mass swelled to the height of a man, each tendril found its mark in the foreheads of the Witchfinder's killers.

"Seth." Simon's voice quaked. "Seth, let's be gone. Please."

No words formed on Seth's lips, although he felt them move. He took a step forward and stopped. Each of the men stood perfectly still, each linked to the black fog by a tendril. Seth motioned to Simon to get down.

"I can save one of them, at least. Maybe he can tell us what that thing is." Seth moved forward.

"Seth, no."

Seth waved away Simon's concern. Whatever held these men, it seemed fully occupied. There were no spare tendrils waving in the air, so it should be safe to approach. Seth took cautious steps toward the group.

On the opposite side of the Witchfinder's corpse, one of the men opened his mouth. Seth paused, but the man did not speak. His tongue, swollen with blood, forced open his jaw and protruded. His eyes widened, swelled and burst. The man's skin shriveled.

Another of the men opened his mouth, then another. Eyes popped, skin withered and fell away in dry, parchment sheets.

Muscles wasted, pot bellies retracted, red-streaked bone showed through faces peeled by decay. Seth grabbed the nearest man and pulled back. The man's arms came away at the shoulders. Seth dropped the arms and stared at them, watched as the accelerated decomposition liquefied the flesh.

Ten men hung like wasted puppets from black threads of smoke. The mass pulled back its tendrils. Ten skeletal bodies hit the ground in a clatter of bone. Seth backed away. The mass formed new filaments and lashed at the air.

"Run. For God's sake, run." Simon shouted again, from directly behind Seth. The mass became still, then threw all its filaments at Seth. There was no time to run, the threads struck with the speed of a viper.

There was no pain, just an intense cold. Seth tried to pull away but the filaments pierced his skin, followed by more, thicker black tendrils. Behind him, Simon shrieked. The black shape pulled itself closer, shortening its tendrils as it approached.

Seth's heart pounded, his intestines churned as the floating darkness hovered in front of him. It paused for a moment, and then shot into him, firing frozen darts into every inch of his skin. A primal terror tore at him, rending his soul, feeding on his memories. The presence, now within him, ripped at his being. It absorbed all that he was, all he had ever been. Summoning the last shred of his own volition, Seth spoke.

"Simon. Get away."

Seth's mind surrendered to a new owner. His thoughts, his memories blended and faded until at last the invader showed itself to him. The darkness laughed while it threaded through nerve and sinew, skin and bone. Seth fell into oblivion. His soul lost its independent existence to become a footnote in the thousands of years of accumulated thought that was the Golab.

Chapter Twenty-Four

"So, you have made your decision." Demdike stood in front of Jessica and picked at his teeth. She was bound to a table in his tower, left there by Lord West and his men.

There had been no argument, little discussion. Demdike had given instructions and his Lordship followed them, meek as a puppy. The sight had horrified Jessica, the pain and apology in Lord West's eyes as though he were powerless, a mere pawn for Demdike's will.

Now she was spread-eagled on her back, wrists and ankles bound with rope. Normal rope, not magical chains this time. If Demdike could be induced to leave her, she had the means to free herself. Jessica raised her head.

"You know I cannot join you. I work alone, and only for the benefit of others. You are interested only in your own ambition."

"True." Demdike moved around the table. His thin hand peeled Jessica's wet dress from her legs. "You will help me achieve that ambition, willingly or otherwise." His fingers delved between her legs, pressing and searching. Jessica fought the ropes, shouting her indignation.

"Filthy swine! Take your hands off me!"

"There is no need for alarm. I merely wish to check your value." Demdike pulled Jessica's dress back over her legs. "You are a virgin, Jessica Chadwick. Good. You will make a fine gift."

"What are you talking about, monster?"

"That will become clear in due course. Tell me, why have you rejected the ways of your ancestors? In your veins, the blood of Chattox flows like fire, yet you hold it down, quashing its desire. Why?"

"I will not go that way. My great-aunt was evil. I am not."

Demdike shrugged. "No matter. I had hoped you would combine your powers with mine willingly, but I see I have to extract them by force. A little more effort, but the end result will be the same." He moved to a table set against the wall, above Jessica's head. She wriggled until she could see what he was doing. The table was draped in black cloth, embroidered in silver with symbols, a few of which she recognized. This was an altar, dedicated to something very dark. Baal.

"You cannot take my power by force. It is worthless unless freely given."

"What a quaint notion." Demdike picked up a long curved dagger. "Some ridiculous idea of your mother's, perhaps?" He moved past Jessica and placed the dagger on the table beside her, adjusting its position until he nodded in satisfaction.

"You place too much credence in romantic tales, Jessica. I assure you, you are of considerable value, both to myself and to my patron. Whether you are a willing accomplice or merely a victim is of little consequence. It will not affect the outcome."

"Then why ask me to join you? Why not just kill me immediately?"

Demdike walked back to the altar. "It would have been easier if you were willing. The final ceremony will be difficult to perform alone, but I'm sure I will manage."

"You think this is your final ceremony?" Jessica tugged at the ropes. They were too tight to slip her hands through. She needed an opportunity to use her unraveling spell.

"No. This is yours, Jessica. I'm afraid you will not witness my final ceremony after all." Demdike sighed. "It would have been good to have a partner. Someone with whom I could share intelligent conversation. Most of these people have spent so long in the company of farm animals, they have begun to think like them."

He took a brass bowl from the altar and placed it on the table, on the left side of Jessica's body, opposite the knife.

"You think you will become *Harab-Serapel*? You will not. Baal is playing with you, Demdike. You are an amusement to him." She stopped when Demdike slapped her, his nails raking her cheek.

"Oh, now look what you have caused me to do." He tutted as he wiped blood from her cheek with the edge of his robe. The stench of decay roared into her nostrils, making her retch. Demdike moved back to the altar.

"You are wrong, though I wonder that you know so much." He folded his arms and stared down at her. "Baal is my patron. I have given him eyes, tongues, hearts and blood, animals, and lately, humans. He has preserved me through the long years. When I asked, he sent Sabnock to build this tower. I have only to request it, and Gaap will move it to any place I please.

"My power I dedicate to his use, and when I absorb your mind, my power will double. Then it will be enough. I will join the

Harab-Serapel and bring death to all who resist him." He cradled her head in his hands and brought his face close to hers. His breath, like the gas from an open latrine, burned her eyes.

"Jessica, I will have your mind when it is driven from you." Demdike released her face and turned again to the altar.

"You can't kill me, Demdike. If you do, my soul will be free. You cannot be executioner if you are to be the recipient of this magic." Jessica stared at the ceiling, wondering how she could know this.

Laughing, Demdike placed black candles on the table around her. "The blood of Chattox brings memories, I see. Next you will want to collect fingers and heads, as your great-aunt once did."

He snapped his fingers, and all the candles ignited. "You are right. I will be the vessel, symbolized by the bowl on your left. Your executioner will thrust the knife into your right side. I will drink your life from the bowl."

"I will resist you. This will be no easy spell."

"Fight, if you wish. You slipped my chains once before, but these ropes are secure. I think you will find, also, that your mind will fail when your executioner arrives. It will be driven from you, and it will be mine. Your soul will be my gift to Baal, the gift that will secure his favor."

Demdike lifted a large book from the altar and stood on Jessica's left. He opened it and turned pages covered with drawings of twisted, deformed plants, decorated tubes, strange nymphs and intricate patterns.

Jessica strained to see the writing but it was too small to read at that distance. Demdike placed his finger on one page and read aloud in a deep, monotonous tone. Jessica wondered what Foras and the others were doing. They had saved her from Demdike once before. Why not now?

The language Demdike spoke was unfamiliar to Jessica but it carried sounds of terror, of things vile and creeping. Shapeless, nameless things, depraved and loathsome, writhed in those words. Jessica cried out when one familiar word issued from Demdike's drone.

Harab-Serapel. Demdike was calling forth a Raven of Death.

Chapter Twenty-Five

Simon pulled the tarpaulin over himself and held his breath. He peered from beneath its folds at Seth, who had fallen to his knees. Simon's stomach wanted to reject his meal of stew, but he swallowed hard against the rising in his throat.

The darkness was now entirely within Seth's body. Seth stood and took a few halting steps. He raised his arms and examined them, flexed his muscles, clenched his fists.

"This will do. It is the best of this bunch, I think." There was a booming quality to Seth's voice that had not been there before. A confident, strident voice, unlike the quiet-spoken Seth Crocker that Simon knew.

"I will have my witch now. I will drink her pain, taste her fear." Seth lifted his open hands to the sky. "And at the last, I will feed on her death. The strength of her life will nourish me."

Simon clenched his teeth to prevent himself crying out. Seth ran for the road. He passed the cart but ignored both it and Simon. His feet pounded the earth as he ran along the road Lord West had taken.

The trembling in Simon's limbs was so intense he felt sure the whole cart shook. He drew a long, shuddering breath and held himself as still as he could. Seth—or whatever Seth had become— must be heading for Demdike's tower. Simon could not keep up on foot. He had to try to drive the cart, although he had no idea how.

Tears formed in his eyes as he realized the futility of what he intended to do. Simon was far too weak to fight Seth or Demdike now, not that he had ever been strong enough to beat either of them alone. The black thing in Seth had killed ten men, and Demdike had killed trained soldiers. Simon lay beneath his tarpaulin and cried.

The horses whinnied and snorted. Simon stilled his sobs and listened. Someone was coming. Simon wiped his eyes and lay motionless.

"Well, this is all turning into a bit of a mess. It has a stronger body now." The high, sibilant voice seemed to come from the ground.

"We are fortunate it has not taken Nicholas Demdike." A deeper voice, too close for comfort.

"Fortunate indeed, but the creature will go after Demdike now. He has Jessica, and it was his influence that turned these people into murderers." A third voice, hoarse and throaty. "The thing will want revenge."

The sibilant voice spoke again. This time it sounded as though it was beneath the cart. "Seere and Crocell have returned to tell Foras what has happened. Foras will probably forbid interference, so we must move quickly before he tells us not to."

The throaty voice laughed. "Bifrons, it is not simply Foras's word that forbids interference. Have you forgotten why we are here?"

"I have not. However, we are indebted to the witch, and the trap cannot work without her. Besides, we must not allow Demdike to try to kill the Golab."

Simon tried to make sense of the conversation but could not. The name of Foras was familiar; he had heard Elizabeth mention it. Did Jessica have two demons? Something landed on the back of the cart, something small. Simon held his breath.

"We can make use of this cart." The deep voice again. "If she does escape, she might be hurt. We will need something to carry her. It is a good thing I was close enough to calm these horses, or they might have bolted and hurt themselves."

The cart lurched as the speaker climbed into the seat. Simon curled his fingers. Whatever was in the cart walked across Simon's back, toward his head. It mewed and pulled at the tarpaulin.

"What is it, Belson?" The throaty voice spoke. Simon bit his lip. The tarpaulin lifted away. Simon blinked in the sunlight.

"It is a man." The throaty voice issued from a face that looked more cat than human. A mane of yellow-orange hair surrounded a face with a protruding snout, lips drawn back over long teeth that could have been smiling or snarling. The head rested on a humanlike body, clad in red leather armor. Thick yellow hair covered every inch of exposed flesh. The creature held the tarpaulin in one hand, while the other rested on the hilt of a long sword at its side. Simon raised his hands to protect his face.

"It looks broken." The deep voice belonged to a man with a long head, the head of a horse. Simon whimpered. The horse head shook. "We should not be seen. Foras will be angry."

"Oh, Foras this, Foras that." The sibilant voice came from the end of the cart, where the tarpaulin obscured Simon's view. "It is too late to worry about small details. The Golab will fight Demdike, and the outcome will not be good either way. Remember, all this is partly our fault. We must put things right."

The cat-headed creature held its hand out to Simon. Simon drew back. He tried to speak but what came out was somewhere between a whine and a cough.

"You need not fear us. We intend no harm," the horse-headed creature said.

Belson rubbed against Simon's arm. Grateful for the presence of something within his understanding, Simon stroked the cat. Belson purred.

"It seems Belson knows you, Simon Bulcock. You are a friend to Jessica Chadwick, the witch who has given us our opportunity." The cat-creature bared its fangs again. "I am Alloces. Please, stand up."

"You know my name?" Simon found his hand reaching for the creature's, apparently of its own accord.

"Belson knows you." Alloces took Simon's hand and pulled him upright. He dropped the tarpaulin.

"I am Orobas." The horse-head tilted to one side. "You were the man in the wooden punishment device. The one Jessica tried to release."

Simon's head reeled. He grabbed at the side of the cart for support.

"These experiences have been too much for him. His mind cannot cope." The sibilant voice sounded at Simon's feet. He looked down and screamed. The head with spider legs bared thin, pointed teeth in a hideous grin.

The world spun around Simon. Sounds drifted in and out of reality. The river's gentle gurgle became a roar. His mind flashed images of Demdike, of skinned soldiers, of Daniel being torn apart, of ten men sucked dry by fog, of Seth becoming possessed...

Simon passed from consciousness, and welcomed the darkness as it enveloped his thoughts.

Chapter Twenty-Six

The bang sounded close, as though something battered against the tower. Demdike seemed not to hear it. The bang repeated. Demdike continued his chant, unmoved.

The air thickened, its background stench overwhelmed by the reek of freshly-spilled entrails. Jessica wrinkled her nose. She had experienced this in her own kitchen, when cleaning rabbits, but it had been a light odor, easily dissipated. Here, it gave the impression of something much larger being disemboweled.

A faint mist developed to Jessica's right. Twisting in time with the rhythm of Demdike's voice, it gradually coalesced. Jessica's throat constricted. The thing forming there was big, with too many limbs. She balled her hands into fists and closed her eyes, concentrating on the unraveling spell that would get her out of the ropes.

Another bang made her open her eyes. Jessica noticed a twitch in Demdike's lip as he read. He must have heard it, and it had nothing to do with the spell he chanted. Glancing right, she saw the demon approach solidity. It was still transparent, but the long snout, the multiple eyes, black wings and rows of arms were clear. This was the form Demdike aspired to reach. This was a *Harab-Serapel*.

Her time was up. She started the words of her spell.

The next bang was followed by a crash and a roar, then footsteps as someone—or something—ran into the hallway. The ropes on Jessica's wrists frayed. Demdike's voice quavered. The *Harab-Serapel* growled, faded then reformed.

"Demdike! Come out, you worthless skeleton." The voice bellowed, interspersed with the sounds of doors opening. Jessica held her breath, stopping her spell for a moment. She could not place the voice, but it certainly wasn't Foras. She resumed her spell.

The door swung open and crashed against the wall. A large man strode into the room, his face contorted in rage. He fixed his gaze on Jessica.

"My witch. Mine." He started toward her. Jessica recognized

him as the man from the cart, the one who had delivered her to Demdike yesterday. The one called Seth.

Demdike faltered then fell silent. The *Harab-Serapel* dissipated, howling, into the air. Demdike shrieked.

"How dare you enter here?" He dropped the book and moved his arms in rapid arcs through the air. "I should have included you in Featherstone's fate. It was a mistake to spare you, but it will take only a moment to rectify that error."

"You turned them against me, you strip of dried meat." Seth raised his fists.

"Against you?" Demdike hesitated. His arms stopped moving. "I did nothing to you, peasant. However, I am about to." He grinned at Jessica. "This will not take long."

Seth struck with speed and agility. Demdike flew backwards. He hit the wall and slid into a sitting position.

"Die, creature, and return the witch you stole." Seth crossed the room to where Demdike climbed to his feet. Demdike made rapid motions with his hands.

"Now you will suffer. No quick death, no easy route to Hell for you." Green fire erupted, covering Demdike's arms.

Jessica continued her spell. The ropes around her wrists and ankles loosened as their fibers separated. Seth halted and bared his teeth at Demdike.

The fire gathered into a ball, which moved along Demdike's arms to hover in the air between his hands. Demdike hissed and the ball shot forwards, catching Seth in the chest. He flew backwards and hit the altar. Bowls overturned and spilled decaying meat onto the floor. Jessica winced at the sound of cracking ribs but continued her spell. Seth regained his balance, grinning.

Demdike gasped.

"Not so easy, eh?" Seth spat blood as he spoke. "If you should succeed in killing me, the consequences for you are terrible indeed."

The bonds holding Jessica broke as Demdike moved toward Seth. She lay still, watching. Yesterday this man had handed her to Demdike. Now he seemed to want her for himself. Perhaps he was possessed by one of the demons in her house? Yet Foras told her they could not interfere in human lives.

Demdike spoke a few words in a guttural language. A shaft of darkness flew from his outstretched hand and pierced Seth's chest. Seth howled in pain and fury. His body darkened and sent black filaments whipping through the air.

Jessica slid off the table, sending the bowl clattering to the floor. Demdike spun around, hissing. One of Seth's filaments encircled Demdike's head, its tip diving under his cowl. Demdike shrieked.

Jessica's knee pressed against something as she cowered beside the table. She looked down at the book. On an impulse, she grabbed it and clutched it to her chest.

Life faded in Seth's eyes, but the darkness growing from him increased as he sank to his knees, then to the floor. Demdike grabbed at the black tendril reaching into his cowl, screaming his rage. More of the tendrils flowed from the dark shape that formed above Seth's body. The shapeless black mass detached from Seth and hovered in the air for a moment before following its tendrils to Demdike.

Jessica's eyelids stretched wide. She forced herself to blink since the dryness of her eyes was hurting. Something so primal, so unformed, so—unmade, could only be one creature. This was the true form of the Golab. Somehow it had moved from the Witchfinder into Seth, and now it was transferring itself to Demdike. Still clutching the book, Jessica ran from the room.

The main door lay broken, hanging from one hinge. She ducked around it into the late afternoon sunlight and ran, cringing at the screams from the tower but not daring to look back.

Chapter Twenty-Seven

Simon woke to the gentle rocking of the cart. He lay with his eyes closed, hoping that when he opened them he would see Daniel seated beside him, and Seth in the driver's seat. The horrors in his memory must have been dreams, brought on by Miriam's overdone stew. They should be close to the mill pond by now. He hoped they were in time to save Jessica. A hoarse voice shocked Simon into opening his eyes.

"There she is."

Simon faced Alloces, who stared ahead of the cart. Simon sat up and followed his gaze. Jessica ran from the open door of Demdike's tower.

"Jessica," he called. "Over here." Simon made to lean over the front of the cart but recoiled at the sight of the top of Bifrons' head. Orobas whinnied. The cart rode onto the grass beside the road and turned around.

Simon blinked. Orobas held no reins. The horses pulling the cart had no bridles.

Alloces moved to the rear of the cart and hauled Jessica aboard. She dropped a large book onto the boards. The cart moved forward.

"It is good to see you have escaped unharmed." Bifrons climbed into the back of the cart. Simon pressed himself into a corner and shuddered.

"No thanks to you." Jessica glared at the little demon. "I was nearly killed." She lifted Belson and stroked his fur. He pressed his head against her chest.

"We were on our way to help." Bifrons folded his tiny arms. "We took this cart in case you needed it, but I see you do not." He seemed overly interested in what Belson was doing.

"Yes, I do. We must get back to the house. The Golab has changed to a new body, and now it is taking Demdike's."

Orobas whinnied again. The cart moved faster.

"It could be worse," Alloces said. "Although not very much worse."

Jessica's gaze met Simon's. He managed a weak smile.

"Simon. You are alive." Jessica crawled along the boards of the bouncing cart to where Simon cowered. "Thank God."

"I think I am alive, but I am probably mad. I see heads on legs, men with the heads of animals, and I have seen men die in awful ways." Simon took Jessica's hands in his. "Jessica, what are these things? What have you called down upon us?"

Jessica lowered her head. Her hair fell forward to hide her face. "What I have called, I called for my own defense. The consequences are more than I could have foreseen." She tightened her grip on his fingers. Simon winced in pain and sucked in air. Jessica looked up. She released his hands and brushed her hair back from her face.

"Simon, you are in pain. When we get to my house, I have some herbs that will help."

"Regrettably, there will not be time." Alloces stood over them. "The Golab will follow us." He bared his teeth at Jessica. "We have not met. I am Alloces."

"Golab." Simon rubbed his hands together to ease their pain. "What is this Golab? The head-thing mentioned it once before. Is it the black fog that took Seth?"

Bifrons appeared at Alloces' feet. He held his nose high, and his grin had vanished. "The head-thing has a name, Simon Bulcock." Bifrons swayed with the motion of the cart. "I am Bifrons, and an Earl. I expect a little respect."

Simon started to bluster an apology. Jessica giggled. Bifrons' lip twitched. Alloces turned away. From the front of the cart, Orobas snickered.

The cart hit a pothole and jolted sideways. Jessica fell backwards. Simon grabbed at the sides of the cart, but the jolt lifted his backside from the boards before slamming him back down.

Orobas made frantic sounds, but the cart was clearly beyond his control. It hit another pothole and tipped over. The horses screamed. Simon lost his grip and slid from the cart to roll along the grass verge. Jessica landed beside him. Bifrons was catapulted into the air.

Simon watched in horror as the spider-legs writhed above him, and closed his eyes when it seemed the thing was heading his way. Something heavy landed on his chest and knocked the breath from his lungs. Simon kept his eyes closed and hoped the hideous monster would climb off him of its own accord. He did not want to have to touch it.

The cart groaned, wood splintered and cracked, and over this noise was the voice of Orobas, calling to the horses. Simon lay still until the noise stopped. Even then he dared not open his eyes in case he came face to face with Bifrons. The thing on his chest made no movement.

"Are you both unhurt?" Alloces' throaty voice broke the silence. "Bifrons, get off there." The last comment ended with a chuckle, and the weight disappeared from Simon's chest. He opened his eyes. Alloces stood over him, lifting the heavy book Jessica had carried from Demdike's tower. Simon blew a relieved breath. It had been the book on his chest.

Bifrons buried his face between Jessica's breasts. She pushed him off and sat up, brushing at her skirt. She glared at the little demon and adjusted her dress. Bifrons waggled his eyebrows at Simon. He strutted away on his thin legs to where the cart lay on its side.

Simon accepted Alloces' hand and stood. His legs threatened to buckle under him, so he placed his feet far apart and stood still. Jessica took his arm. She carried the book Alloces had lifted from his chest.

"What do we do now?" Jessica's voice cracked. "We have to get back to the house before the Golab catches up."

Orobas had released the horses from their harness. They followed him to where the cart's occupants stood. Jessica scanned the ground.

"Where is Belson?" She smiled at the black shape that walked from the tall grass, his tail held high and bristling with indignation.

Orobas opened his mouth to speak. He covered it with his hand to disguise a laugh.

"My apologies," he said. "I lost my concentration for a moment." He chuckled again.

Simon narrowed his eyes. He failed to see what was funny in this situation.

"Can you ride a horse?" Orobas spoke directly to Simon, who shook his head.

"One of us could fetch Seere." Bifrons picked over the shattered remains of a wheel. "Orobas, you are the fastest."

"Seere cannot take us all at once." Orobas ran his tongue over his lips. "We must all be present when the Golab arrives."

"I still don't know what this Golab is," Simon said. Orobas motioned him to silence.

"Alloces, take this horse and ride for the house." Orobas nodded to one of the horses, which stepped forward and stood patiently beside Alloces. Alloces mounted, and the horse set off at a gallop. Orobas turned his attention to Bifrons.

"Bifrons, you can take the other." Orobas motioned to the other horse, which shook its head and snorted. Orobas rolled his eyes. He cupped his hand over the horse's ear and whispered into it. The horse snickered and nodded, but still eyed Bifrons warily as Orobas lifted him onto its back, along with Belson. Bifrons gave Jessica one last leer before the horse broke into a gallop.

Simon breathed his relief at being rid of the revolting creature, but the sight of Orobas dropping to all fours, then swelling into a large white horse shook his senses. His knees gave way. Only Jessica's support prevented Simon crashing to the ground. He landed on his knees.

"I can't take much more of this." Simon let his head slump forward.

"There is not much more to take. One way or the other, this will end tonight."

Orobas nudged Simon with his snout. Jessica pulled at his arm. Simon stood and faced the gathering twilight. He allowed Jessica to help him onto Orobas's back. She climbed up behind him and stretched her arms around his chest. Simon felt the hard shape of the book press into his back. He had seen that book in Demdike's hands, and its presence chilled him now. Simon took hold of Orobas's mane.

"I will travel fast, but have no fear. I will not let you fall." Orobas snickered. He muttered 'head-thing' to himself then shot forward. Simon closed his eyes and bared his teeth into the wind.

Chapter Twenty-Eight

Even through the heavy book, Jessica felt the pounding of Simon's heart and the tremble in his body. She had grown up with magic, but the results of her conjuration of Foras terrified her. It amazed Jessica that Simon had not been driven insane by today's events. She drew a sharp breath when she remembered her house. How would he react to that?

They passed Bifrons in the gathering darkness, and reached the house just as Alloces dismounted. Orobas sank to his knees to let Jessica and Simon climb down. He reared and assumed his almost-human form.

Bifrons' horse reached the house and stopped dead, its head lowered. Bifrons shot over the horse's head. He landed upside-down in the grass beside the house. The horse whinnied until Orobas picked Belson's claws from its back.

"Infernal creature. It did that on purpose." Bifrons spat grass. He picked a beetle from his ear and threw it aside.

"I had to let the horse do that to Bifrons." Orobas whispered to Jessica. "It was the only way I could persuade him to take the 'head-thing' at all." He chuckled before adding. "Bifrons is made of stern stuff. His pride is the only thing hurt, and he will soon forget. Besides, it will take a century for him to live down the indignity of being referred to as 'the head-thing.'"

Orobas spoke to the horses. They nodded to him before running along the road, disappearing into the darkness.

Jessica opened the door to her house. She glanced at Simon, then stepped inside. Belson nearly tripped her in his rush to enter.

Alloces passed Jessica in the hallway. He turned to the right and opened the door set into the wall. Foras was inside, talking with Andromalius and Phenex.

Still clutching the book, Jessica ran to Foras. "Where were you? I had to escape on my own." She held the book to her chest and glared at him.

A hint of a smile touched Foras's lips. "You are perfectly capable of escaping from Demdike. When he took you from the Golab, my concern was eased. Did you use your flare, or have you found deeper magic?"

"I was lucky, that's all. The Golab burst in just as Demdike called a *Harab-Serapel*."

The smile dropped from Foras's face. His eyes glowed green. "What has happened? Tell me, in detail, and quickly."

Bifrons ran up the wall and stopped at eye level. "We saw the Witchfinder killed at the river. The villagers did it, after Demdike left with Jessica. The Golab emerged. It killed everyone except two men. One it possessed, the other was hiding."

Foras met Bifrons' eyes. "The hidden man did not see you, I hope?"

"Ah." Bifrons inclined his head toward the door. "We brought him with us. He is a friend of Jessica's."

Foras pressed the heels of his hands to his forehead. He took a deep breath before facing Simon, who stood with a blank expression on his face, between Orobas and Alloces.

With Foras distracted from her attention, Jessica realized the room she was in shouldn't exist. From outside, her house looked the same as always, so the door they had just passed through should have taken them outside again, to the south of the house. Instead, the door led to a large room, decorated with paneling like the hallway. Two wide windows looked out over the darkness of the road, and another on the opposite wall must show the garden. Beside this, in the new south wall, was yet another door.

A large padded sofa was set against one wall. Belson lay curled on this, beside the seated Seere. Another soft chair was occupied by an old man in rust-red leather. Jessica returned his smile and wondered if this were yet another new demon, or another form of one she had already met.

Foras stared at Simon, who was flanked by Orobas and Alloces. Bifrons hung from the wall. Seere spoke with Marchosias and Amon, neither of whom was built for sitting on chairs. Phenex and Andromalius stood beside her. Crocell leaned against a tall chest of drawers. That made eleven. Jessica checked the room, but Malphas was nowhere to be seen. Perhaps the old man in red was one of his forms? Phenex had said there were twelve demons, but she had not yet seen all twelve at once.

Simon whimpered. Jessica forgot her tally and remembered her friend. Simon had been in her house two nights ago, and must be confused. She moved to pass Foras, but he stopped her with one outstretched arm. Foras's stare was fixed on Simon's.

"What is this, Foras? Simon can be trusted. I've known him all my life." Jessica flinched at the hard look on Foras's face.

"I sensed deception in this one, when he came to your door. I cannot find it now." Foras kept his gaze locked with Simon's. "I must be sure of him. He bears the taint of dark power, a power I now know to be Demdike's. If he has told Demdike of our scheme, our trap is futile."

"Simon?" Jessica's eyes widened. "You are mistaken, Foras. Without Simon, I might not have survived here. Let him speak. Release your hold on him."

"Very well." Foras broke the bond that tied his hypnotic stare to Simon's. "Andromalius will know if he speaks the truth. I warn you, Simon Bulcock, not to attempt to lie."

Simon staggered backwards into Alloces, who held him upright. Andromalius stood between Foras and Simon, with his snake held close to Simon's face.

"I don't understand." Simon stared at the snake. "Jessica, what is happening? Where is this place?"

"Don't be frightened, Simon. Just tell Foras how you have helped and supported me since my mother's death, and since my father's capture." Jessica tried to move to Simon's side, but Foras held her back. The book she held was heavy, and her arms hurt with the effort of supporting it.

Simon's gaze darted from one to the other. Jessica hoped he had not lost his mind.

"Speak." Foras's voice deepened. "Tell us why I see Demdike's magic in you."

"It's in us all." Simon almost shrieked the words. "The whole village. Lord West too. Demdike cast a spell over us." Simon's body shook. A thin line of drool fell from the corner of his mouth.

"I believed he wanted to help Jessica. I thought I had betrayed Jessica's mother, I thought I had let the soldiers take her father. It was him. He bewitched me. Everyone else too." Simon cackled and bit into his lip. "Elizabeth helped me. I escaped Demdike's spell. Seth too, he saw through it. I think Daniel would have, if he had not..."

Simon's head drooped onto his chest. Tears dripped onto his shirt. His chest heaved with sobs. "Dan, Seth, Robert. Dead. Because of Demdike and that other thing, Golab, everyone will die."

Foras pulled Simon's head up by the hair. "Not everyone. Tell me how much Demdike knows of us. What does he know of the Golab?"

"Nothing," Jessica shouted. "He didn't know what the Golab was when it came into his tower. He thought he was killing a man." Simon had been through so much, and now Foras acted as though he were some kind of spy. "Orobas, stop this. You defended me once before. Defend Simon."

"I cannot." Orobas moved beside Jessica. The demons had gathered around the group. Phenex touched Jessica's arm.

"Foras is right," Phenex said. "We must be sure of him, but that does not mean we accuse him. If Demdike influenced your friend, he may pose a risk to our plan, even if he does not realize it."

"I don't think he knows anything about you." Simon whispered the words. "He called the Witchfinder here to force Jessica to choose. Demdike sent me to fetch him, but I was caught and put into the pillory. He planned for Jessica to choose between death at the Witchfinder's hands or corruption at his own." Simon turned red-rimmed eyes to Jessica. "I'm sorry. I thought he wanted to help you. I didn't know."

"He speaks the truth." Andromalius draped his snake around his shoulders once more. "If Demdike knows of us, he has not told this man."

"That is something, at least." Foras let Simon's head fall forward. "If Demdike knew of us, then the Golab would have that knowledge when it took his mind."

Jessica took a step backwards, still staring at Simon. She could not believe he had been working for Demdike all this time. The only man she trusted, her only true friend, had conspired with the creature who tried to kill her.

Foras grabbed her shoulder. Startled, she looked into his eyes. Their green glow soothed her, his cinnamon scent calmed her rising anger.

"You say you saw a *Harab-Serapel*? If you did, then it saw you. It may also have seen the Golab."

"Yes." Jessica breathed the word. "It vanished when the Golab interrupted Demdike's spell."

"Then Baal will know of you, at least. Demdike will fight the creature's attempt at possession, but he will lose. His power will give us a little time, but not much. Then the Golab will have Demdike's knowledge and power. It may attempt to call another *Harab-Serapel*. Indeed, it may already have done so."

The edges of the book pressed into Jessica's arms. She held it out to Foras. "Not without this. It's the book Demdike used for his incantation."

Frowning, Foras took the book from her and opened it, flipping through its pages. "You took this from Demdike?"

"While he was fighting Seth." Responding to Foras's quizzical look, Jessica continued. "The Golab was in a man called Seth."

"I see." Foras turned a few more pages. "It is a good thing you did. The power in this book would increase the danger a hundredfold, if the Golab had access to it." He glanced around the room. "Where is Malphas?"

"Building, of course." Phenex moved to the door. "I know where he is. I'll fetch him."

Simon hung limp in Alloces' arms. Jessica could not look at the gray-haired poacher for long. When she thought of Demdike touching her, and realized that Simon had played some part in that, it made her sick.

"All of you, go to the trap and prepare. Take the man with you, he will be no safer here than there. Also, it is better to keep him where we can watch him." Foras closed the book and picked up another from a low table beside the wall. Jessica recognized it as Goetia.

"Belson—" Foras groaned at the sleeping cat. "Belson!" The cat opened its eyes and stretched. "You stand watch. Run to the others at the trap when you see the Golab coming." Foras took a step forward. "Jessica, come with me."

"Where are you going, Foras? The Golab will arrive at any moment." Bifrons scuttled to the floor.

"I have to speak to Baal, to clear our path with him before we act."

"It is dangerous, Foras. Baal is unpredictable and vengeful. He may not take well to the loss of his plaything," Marchosias said.

Foras sighed. "I know. There may be a way to gain his favor though."

"Why expose Jessica to this? She will be vulnerable." Orobas looked at Jessica with his soft, brown eyes.

"She has seen a *Harab-Serapel*. It saw her, so Baal already knows of her existence, but not of our involvement. Jessica is the link between ourselves and Demdike. Without her presence, Baal will suspect deception."

He raised his arm, holding the large book aloft with one hand. "The shreds of Demdike's mind will tell the Golab of this book. With it, the creature can call others of the Unmade. It will come here, for this as much as for Jessica."

The demons murmured among themselves as they filed

through the door into the hallway.

Jessica stood in front of Foras. "What is that book?"

Lowering his arm, Foras turned his attention to her. "We must go into the circle. It seems your petulant insistence on the inclusion of all the sigils will be useful after all."

Malphas' black beak appeared in the doorway, followed by his feathered head and beady eyes. "What is it, Foras? I have bricks to lay."

Where? How big does the house need to be? Jessica hoped Malphas had not built over her new herb garden.

"Take this book, and hide it within the fabric of the house." Foras handed Demdike's book to Malphas. "Then join the others below. Our trap is about to be sprung."

Chapter Twenty-Nine

Simon stared into the abyss. The darkness beckoned with jet-black eyes and ebony threads. It would be so easy to step off, to fall without ever reaching the bottom of that canyon. So much easier than going back. One step forward would end it all.

The images in his mind held no color or substance any more. Thin, wasted pictures of a futile life. Simon, the poacher, to whom the concept of an honest day's work held no meaning and no allure, had moved from being Demdike's unwitting slave to the plaything of demons. What next? Was there any further debasement he could reach?

Something lifted his legs. Through a haze of half-awareness, Simon registered that he was being carried down a flight of stairs. His mind-self chortled. He had never imagined Hell had a stairway. Simon resumed his consideration of the abyss. It promised everything and nothing. No pain, no pleasure. No cold, no warmth. Neither sound nor silence. Oblivion.

"Simon."

The voice came from within himself, and from behind. Elizabeth's voice. Simon could not face her.

"Simon. Step back from the edge." Elizabeth sounded concerned. Simon could see no reason for this. He faced an ending, the quiet comfort of nothing.

"Simon, please. Jessica needs you."

"I failed her." Simon spoke into the abyss. "She hates me now." He thought of Jessica's expression when he revealed himself as Demdike's pawn. Disappointment, disgust, contempt flew over her features. Simon wished the darkness below would rise and take him. It would free him from the decision to jump.

"You have not failed. She will need you, and soon. Simon, you must not take refuge in madness. The abyss is in your mind, it means the end of thought, not life. Step back, Simon. What you face there is a living death."

The darkness writhed in anger at her words. It calmed, pleading without sound to Simon. *Jump*, it said. *I will catch you. There is nothing here to fear. There is nothing here at all.*

Simon took one step back. The abyss closed with a silent promise of return. Elizabeth's eyes hung in the air before him, filled with sympathy. Her voice drifted across the open expanse of his thoughts.

"You will not fail, Simon. I have faith in you."

The tunnel ran straight ahead, lit with candles along both walls. It took Simon a few moments to realize this was not in his head. Alloces held his left arm, Orobas his right and a luminous child walked before them.

"Where am I?" Simon asked the question before realizing he might not want to know the answer.

"Under the garden." Orobas spoke through tight lips. "It is good that you have not succumbed to madness, as Bifrons feared you might. Nevertheless, you must remain silent."

"What garden? Jessica's little patch? There is no tunnel from Jessica's house. I should know. I helped to build it."

"There is now." Alloces' voice carried the same tension. They stopped at a blank wall, the end of the tunnel. The child faced the wall and spoke an invocation.

Simon glanced back along the tunnel. It seemed full of demons, in an assortment of bodies. Some might pass for human; others resembled no creature he had ever seen. The wall in front of him cracked. Simon gaped as a section of it swung inwards. The little demon stepped back, out of the way.

Within was a huge vaulted chamber. In the centre of the chamber was a ring of flame. Simon closed his eyes. He had arrived at Hell.

Chapter Thirty

"I must have Malphas separate these sections, so the power of the sigils does not mingle." Foras spoke as he strode along the curved corridor, as though discussing the finer points of interior decoration. "Perhaps a glass roof also, so that plants may be grown indoors. I understand such buildings have already been constructed by the wealthy in your land."

Struggling to keep pace, Jessica half-ran alongside him. When Malphas left, Foras had guided her to the far end of the room and through the door which led, as she suspected, into the circle. He had made no more mention of the book he gave to Malphas.

"What about that book, Foras?"

"Oh, that?" Foras assumed a grim expression. "It is one of a pair. Together, they represent enormous power." He smiled. "I know now why Demdike is here. His book calls to its brother. Demdike follows where it leads."

"Its brother is Goetia?" Jessica shot an apprehensive glance at the book Foras carried, as though it might turn into some biting snake at any moment.

"No. Demdike's book is called, as near as your language allows, the Arithmetic of Worlds. Its brother is the Geometry of Lives, and is within the books held by the Monks of Marchway."

"Should we get the other book?"

"That would be unwise. Demdike might not know of its existence, and it would be best if it were kept that way. Bringing it here would risk catastrophe." Foras stopped walking and looked at her. "The combination of Demdike's knowledge with the power and ferocity of the Golab is bad enough. The book you stole from Demdike increases the danger a hundred fold, since the Golab has Demdike's knowledge of its use. Both books, if they fell into the hands of the Golab, would give it unlimited power. The Unmade would take back the Earth, and all created life would cease." He stared into her eyes for a moment then resumed walking.

Jessica hurried to keep up. "Foras, what are these Unmade? How can they take back the Earth when it was never theirs?"

"In Eden, creation was perfect." The green in Foras's eyes took on a bright hue, as though he were recalling fond memories of lost times. "Outside, there should have been nothing. All life should have stayed in Eden."

"It didn't?"

"There was—overspill. Drippings, residues, waste, call it what you will. These leftover shreds of life survived and thrived, ignored by us all. They were irrelevant. We were secure in Eden." Foras stopped.

Jessica ran into him. She drew back reluctantly from his solid warmth. "Tell me more, Foras."

"The wastes of life became the Unmade. Some shapeless, like the Golab. Some with solid form, some even as caricatures of life in Eden. It is all there, in that book. Deformed, hideous plants. Twisted animal and even human forms." Foras stared at her, his lips forming a wry smile.

"Once, giant monsters roamed this land. All the Unmade should have been destroyed before man was cast out of Eden, but some survived. This Golab is one who has learned to prey on humans."

"So there are others?" Fascination gripped Jessica.

"We may talk of this another time, but not now." Foras nodded at a gold emblem, below the window. "There is Baal's sigil." He opened Goetia.

Outside, the sun threw long shadows across the garden. Jessica watched the sky darken as Foras read from Goetia. They stood, not within the circle, nor outside it, but on the line that formed it. Jessica wondered if they were protected here, if Foras would be able to control Baal in this unknown realm of magic. What was magic like, here at the boundary?

A toad hopped into view, seeming to come from the wall below the sigil. Jessica watched its progress, fascinated.

"King Baal, welcome."

Jessica looked from Foras to the toad. There was no mistake. Foras was definitely addressing the toad. She had expected a more impressive manifestation for a King of Hell.

Before she could speak, the toad swelled, bubbled and popped. In its place stood a man, old yet clearly filled with health, his mouth twisted in a sneer. Baal's eyes burned like coals, illuminating the corridor with a blood-red glow. He spoke in a voice that reminded Jessica of Demdike's speech; sweet and low, with an undercurrent of menace. Yet there was something more in that voice, something of malevolent humor, a cruel jester's tone.

"Foras. It has been some time since we met. Have you relinquished your ridiculous quest?"

Foras shook his head. "I, and others, still hope to return to the Host."

"Pointless," Baal laughed, "but entertaining. I enjoy your struggle, Foras." His red eyes turned to Jessica. "Ah, I see you have the virgin Demdike promised me. Why is she still alive?"

"She is not his to give. Baal, I have called you to strike a bargain."

"Bargain?" Baal's voice shook the room. "Demdike is my pet, my toy. This woman was in his grasp. Why should I bargain for what is mine?"

"Demdike has been stolen from you."

Baal pursed his lips. "I know of this. I sent one of my *Harab-Serapel* at his request, but it came back to me unused. Demdike was lost to me after that."

"It was a Golab, Baal. One of Asmodeus's pets. It has taken Demdike's body and consumed his soul."

"Indeed? Then I must have my revenge on Asmodeus." Fire flared in Baal's eyes. Jessica cringed. She moved behind Foras for protection, but was unsure whether he could provide it.

"Your wishes coincide with mine, Baal. I intend to trap this Golab, then kill it. To do this, it will be necessary to destroy the body of Nicholas Demdike." Foras bowed his head. "King Baal, I ask your permission to destroy the body of your servant."

Baal rubbed his chin. The fire in his eyes reduced to a dull glow. "Well, Demdike will provide me with no further entertainment anyway, so you can kill him if you like. I will withhold my *Harab-Serapel* from his use. If you kill the Golab, it will infuriate Asmodeus, and I can tell him of my involvement after the act is completed. I think I will derive sufficient pleasure from his reaction. That leaves the matter of the virgin. I still claim her as mine."

Foras cleared his throat. "She is in my care. What would you require, to relinquish your claim?"

Eyebrows raised, Baal leaned to one side so that he could see Jessica.

"You have formed some attachment to the woman, Foras? This borders on bestiality, you realize?"

"She is in my care." Foras repeated the words through his teeth. "Without her, I would not have this chance to move toward redemption. I cannot repay her with death."

"I see." Baal leered at Jessica. She cowered behind Foras, her heart pounding.

"Well, I have lost the amusement that was Demdike." Baal folded his arms. "I would trade her for a joke." He pointed at Foras. "At your expense. Here is my offer. I will play a joke on you, Foras, and you will not resist me. If you do, her soul is forfeit."

"I accept." Foras tensed. Behind him, Jessica felt the increased heat within his body. His voice sounded as though he were forcing it through tight lips. "I am sure it will be a most amusing diversion."

Baal roared with laughter. "I have already decided what it will be. Very well, Foras, you may keep the woman. I will not aid Demdike if he calls, since his soul is no longer mine, and I will play my joke after you have trapped this Golab. Enjoy your little animal pet. Farewell, Foras, this has been a most entertaining meeting."

Flames spread from Baal's eyes, consumed his face, and spread down his body until he became a column of fire. The column thinned to a red line and disappeared.

Darkness filled the corridor. The sun had set beyond the circle, leaving the sky deep blue tinged with pink. Jessica touched Foras's arm.

"Are we safe now?"

"We are never safe." Foras closed Goetia and started back along the corridor. "I have given Baal leave to perform a joke on me."

"Just a joke, Foras. How bad can it be?" Jessica hurried after him.

"His jokes are cruel, Jessica. Whatever he does, I cannot resist him."

"You will endure, Foras."

Green light flared in Foras's eyes. "I will, yes, but his jokes can have repercussions." Foras waved his hand and candles, placed in sconces around the walls, flared to life. Through the window, the circular corridor lived with light around its entire circumference.

Foras glanced at Jessica. "His joke may not be directed solely at me. Despite his manner, he has not forgotten his claim on you. We may both be victims of his depraved amusements."

Chapter Thirty-One

Simon expected to be flung into the fire. Instead, the demons spread around the circumference of the room. Each took their positions beneath the carved stone images of themselves.

Bifrons, and a giant Simon had heard referred to as Seere, walked the circle, and made signs in the air. One by one, the demons vanished. The demon shaped like a small boy ran back into the tunnel.

Alloces led Simon to a place on the wall, beneath the carved head of Foras. Alloces drew his sword and held its tip to Simon's throat.

"I have no wish to harm you, Simon Bulcock. I realize you do not understand what we are doing. You must find it within yourself to trust us. Make no movement, no sound. Whatever you see happening here, you must let it happen. Do not interfere."

Simon nodded once, without taking his eyes from Alloces' face. Alloces pressed the sword a little harder.

"Believe me, I will kill you before I allow you to destroy our work. Make no sound, Simon Bulcock. All you have to do is stay out of the way."

Simon nodded again. Alloces withdrew his sword and stood back. He regarded Simon for a moment then strode to his own place along the wall.

By the time Bifrons and Seere reached Simon, his terror had subsided a little. Simon still pressed his back to the cool stone of the wall at their approach, but he no longer felt the urge to run. From what Alloces had said, Simon deduced that something very important was about to happen. He was to witness it, and as long as he remained silent he might even live to tell the tale.

The spell Bifrons and Seere cast over him made no difference as far as Simon could tell. He felt nothing, he stood in exactly the same place. Bifrons and Seere moved on. They cast the same spell over Alloces, who faded from sight. Simon glanced down at his feet. He saw himself with perfect clarity. So, the demons weren't leaving. The spell simply made them invisible to others.

Simon flexed his fingers. They tingled but he had movement

again. Strength had returned to his legs. His face, still swollen, ached and throbbed, but it was bearable. Perhaps he had recovered enough to be of some use to Jessica, if he only knew where she was now.

Seere and Bifrons cast their spell over two empty spaces on the wall, then moved to their own places and disappeared. Simon frowned at this. Their reasoning became clear a moment later, when a black crow flew into the chamber, followed by the small boy.

The crow and the boy ducked into the empty spaces and blended with the wall. Simon took a deep breath and stared around the apparently-empty chamber. Whatever the demons planned, it must be imminent.

The flames in the centre of the room died down. Candles ignited around the walls to replace the lost light of the fire. Into this new gloom, from the open tunnel entrance, came the sound of running footsteps.

Chapter Thirty-Two

In the lounge, Foras stopped, a brief look of concentration creasing his features. Within moments, the fluttering of wings announced Malphas's arrival from the hallway. He landed on the floor and assumed nearly-human form.

"Foras. You are just in time. Belson returned moments ago. The Golab is on its way here."

"Good. We are ready."

Foras followed Malphas to the door. "I trust you have hidden the Arithmetic of Worlds securely? It must not be found, even if we fail."

Malphas nodded. He resumed his bird shape and flew into the hallway.

Jessica stepped forward and tapped Goetia. "What about this one?"

"Goetia presents no immediate danger. Besides, when this is over, it should be returned to its owners." Foras placed the book on a chair. Gripping Jessica's arm, firmly but without pressure, he led her to the hallway.

"What now, Foras?" Jessica heard the tremble in her own voice and realized how frightened she was. They stood at the doorway to the cellar, facing the front door of the house.

"We wait." Foras released her arm. "The door is not locked. When it enters, make sure it sees you, and then run into the cellar, along the tunnel. The Golab will follow."

"What will you do?"

"I can delay it for a time, so that it will not overtake you before you reach the chamber. The others will meet you there."

Nausea gripped Jessica's stomach, though she was at a loss to explain it. She had faced the Witchfinder, escaped Demdike and his *Harab-Serapel*, and even survived an audience with Baal, a King of Hell who laid claim to her soul. This was different. Now she waited, as she knew she would eventually have to, as bait for a demon's trap.

If she fell, if the Golab caught her before she reached the end of the tunnel, everything she had endured would have been for nothing. Taking deep breaths, Jessica faced the door, her head high, fists clenched at her sides.

The door opened with a crash, bringing a sweep of chill air into the house. Framed against the darkness outside, Demdike's thin, cowled shape detached itself from the night and moved forward into the hall.

Foras bent close to whisper in Jessica's ear. "It must not know my name. There is still time for it to call on Asmodeus, before it enters the circle."

"Well, Jessica, we meet again. I see you have made use of your witchery after all." Demdike indicated the hallway with a sweep of his bony hand. "You are not above using your powers for your own benefit." Demdike slid closer.

Jessica backed away, moving into the open doorway to the cellar.

Foras stepped between them. "Who is this, Jessica? A knight in shining armor?" The mockery in Demdike's voice infuriated Jessica, while the stench from him revolted her.

"He is—" She caught herself just in time. Searching for a name, she chose the first one that came into her head. "He is William. You cannot pass him."

Demdike threw back his head and laughed. Both of his hands rose to his cowl. He pulled it back to reveal his face.

Jessica screamed.

"Do you think you can stop me, William?" Demdike grinned; black and yellow pointed teeth were visible between cracked, blue lips. His head was hairless, covered in flaking, suppurating skin, and his eyes pure black and lidless. Above the withered remnant of his left ear, the skin bulged, cracked and burst. Yellow-green pus ran down the side of Demdike's head as a white worm wriggled from his flesh.

Even Foras took a step backwards. "Run, Jessica," he said.

Jessica ran.

She took the steps two at a time, too terrified to be concerned about falling. Behind the stair case, the tunnel entrance was open. Phenex waited, his golden glow illuminating the basement. He motioned for her to enter the tunnel.

A scream of unbridled fury echoed from the hallway. Foras must have prevented Demdike's passage. Jessica ran into the tunnel, noting the candles on sconces along both walls. All were lit, but the glow of Phenex overwhelmed their light as he shot past her, racing ahead.

"Wait." The word gasped from Jessica's mouth. "Wait for me."

"I cannot." The answer drifted back on Phenex's gentle voice. "I must prepare. Run, witch. Run as you have never run before."

The tunnel seemed longer than last time. Jessica stopped for breath, judging that she must be over halfway along it by now. There were no markers, no means to judge distance, so she could not be sure. Folding her arms across her chest, she leaned against the wall and forced her ragged breathing to slow. If only she had some of her restorative herbs, but they were behind her now, in the house.

A loud thud sounded behind her. Jessica stared back along the candlelit tunnel, but could see no end to it. The cackle drifting through the darkness spurred her on and she resumed running. It must be Demdike. Somehow he had passed Foras.

Fear overcame fatigue. Jessica ran. Ahead, a blur of light grew as she approached. She glanced behind. Something was running along the ceiling, then the walls.

Demdike. On all fours, he scuttled like a lizard, his darkness blotting out the light from the candles as he passed them. Jessica leaned into her sprint. The bright blur ahead resolved into an open doorway. She shot through and tripped, sprawling on the floor.

Demdike whooped his triumph as he crossed the threshold.

Jessica looked up in time to see the door swing closed, blending with the brickwork, leaving no seam. The fire in the central trough had died. Jessica's head moved in jerks as she scanned the room. Panic pounded at her heart.

There were no demons here. She was alone with the Golab.

Chapter Thirty-Three

Simon clenched his fists. He shifted in his place, but the thought of Alloces' sword at his throat prevented him from rushing to Jessica's aid. She stared around the chamber as she struggled to her hands and knees. Simon bit his lip. Jessica could not know that she was surrounded by invisible demons, and her face showed her fear.

A dark shape climbed from the doorway and clung to the wall. The door closed. Simon pressed his back into the stone. He recognized the shape, which now dropped to the floor and stood erect.

It was Nicholas Demdike. His hood was thrown back to reveal the face Simon had never seen. Now, he could not tear his eyes away from the repulsive sight, though his knees shook with the horror of what he had, until recently, regarded as both teacher and friend.

"Your friend William was strong, but not strong enough." Demdike looked around the chamber. "I must admit I am impressed by your work here, Jessica. This will be a fitting temple for your sacrifice. Asmodeus will be pleased."

Simon had never heard of a William. He had, however, heard of Asmodeus, but Demdike had always followed a master called Baal. He fought the urge to run to Jessica's side when she struggled to her feet and backed away toward the large stone bowl in the centre of the room.

"Last time we met, you wanted to sacrifice me to Baal." Jessica held her head high, but the tremble in her voice betrayed her feelings.

"My master is Asmodeus." Demdike moved forward, his cloak brushing the floor with no apparent motion in his legs. "I can taste your fear already, witch. You will satisfy my hunger, and Asmodeus will reward me for your soul."

He grinned and pointed at Jessica. "You have caused me a great deal of trouble. However, the privacy this place affords will allow me to exact a long and satisfying revenge."

A thin strand of green light whipped from Demdike's fingers and curled around Jessica's ankles. Demdike pulled his hand back. Jessica fell to the floor. She scrambled for the huge stone bowl and used it to pull herself upright. Demdike's green whip coiled in the air.

"I hold the memories of those I ensnare. Did you know that?" Demdike moved closer to Jessica. "I know about your mother's death. And your father's."

"Liar." Jessica ran to the far side of the bowl. She ducked Demdike's whip as it lashed for her face. "You killed my mother, but my father was forced into the army. He might still be alive."

"Ah, you entertain false hope. Let me dispel it for you." Demdike circled, but Jessica kept the stone bowl between them. Demdike's whip lashed the air again.

"Your father has been dead for two years. He died at the battle of Naseby." Demdike grinned at the shock on Jessica's face.

Simon bit into his lip. The pressure of his teeth brought searing pain to his damaged face, but he ignored it. He should have been the one to tell Jessica about her father, but he had never had the courage. Simon stared at the blank walls. Were these demons going to do something, or were they just going to watch?

"No." Jessica shook her head. Tears streamed from her eyes.

Demdike took advantage of her distraction and launched his whip. This time, it raised a red welt across Jessica's forehead. She screamed and clutched at her face.

"You are alone, witch." Demdike moved toward Jessica. He crossed the trench, now devoid of flame, as though he walked on solid ground. "You have nobody."

"That's not true." Jessica circled the stone bowl, staying directly opposite Demdike.

"Are you thinking of William? I have left his charred corpse in your hallway." Demdike traced his finger along the edge of the bowl. "Or perhaps the old poacher, Simon Bulcock? Shall I tell you what he has hidden from you, all these years?"

Simon bit harder. Blood trickled over his chin.

"I don't want to hear your lies. If you are going to kill me, just do it." Jessica screamed at Demdike across the bowl.

He threw back his head and laughed.

"Ah, you are in a hurry, I see. Well, I am not. Your torment delights me, Jessica Chadwick. I have not enjoyed myself so much in centuries." Demdike's whip dissolved into the air.

"There is nothing you can do to frighten me, creature. The villagers have already decided my guilt. Even if I escape you, they will hang me." Jessica curled her lip and shook her hair back.

"Death is certain. I no longer fear it."

"Such delicious irony." Demdike tapped his lips with one finger. "This Demdike killed my host, Matthew Hopkins. Do you not know how?" He tilted his head forward. "It seems you do not. The villagers were in Demdike's thrall. He convinced them that Matthew Hopkins was a dangerous fraud. He stole their memories of your magic."

Demdike laughed. "The villagers think you innocent, but you will not live to see their smiling faces."

Demdike held out one hand, palm upwards. A ball of green flame formed above his fingers. He looked from the ball to Jessica.

"Simon Bulcock knew of your father's death. He kept it from you." Demdike spoke in a low monotone. Jessica gripped the sides of the bowl and lowered her head. Demdike flung the fireball at her.

Jessica shrieked and brought her arm up to cover her face. Demdike's fireball burst against a shield of blue light that covered Jessica's arm.

Demdike inclined his head. "I see you intend to challenge me. Good. It will make your pain last longer." He formed another green ball, bigger than the last.

Simon launched himself forward. He leaped the trench and pushed Jessica aside. Demdike's fire caught his shoulder. Simon tore off his shirt before the corrosive touch of Demdike's magic burned through to his skin.

"Well, Simon Bulcock. Where did you come from?" There was a trace of unease in Demdike's voice. His head scanned the room in a series of jerks. "You seem to have recovered from your ordeal, although your face still bleeds."

"Stay away from her." Simon faced Demdike across the stone bowl. Jessica stood at his side.

"You see, I am not alone." Jessica jutted her chin, and then whispered to Simon, "What are you doing here?"

"I promised your mother I would help you," Simon whispered back. The acoustics of the circular chamber amplified their voices.

"How touching." Demdike clasped his hands beneath his chin. "The valiant poacher comes to the rescue, sneaking and hiding in the shadows." He spread his arms wide. "True, Jessica, you are not alone at this moment, but you will be in the next." Green fire erupted along Demdike's arms. He swung both arms forward and launched a bolt of flame at Simon's chest.

Jessica held out her arm. Her blue shield dispersed most of the blast, but drops of burning green struck Simon's bare chest and shoulders.

Simon's throat constricted. He could make no sound as spiderwebs of agony lanced under his skin. Breathing in ragged gasps, he slapped at his chest and shoulders. Skin peeled from his flesh where the green flame had touched him.

"I do believe I'm going to enjoy this body." Demdike inspected his fingers. "Not the most attractive, and certainly not the strongest I have used, but it has such wonderful capacity to cause pain. The mind, too, feels so attuned to my nature."

Jessica moved to help Simon but he shook his head. He could not bear to think what this vile magic would do to Jessica, if it touched her. Simon raised his head to glare at Demdike.

"Now, Simon, I don't wish to be rude, but Jessica and I have a long night of torture ahead." Demdike formed another fiery green ball. "So if you would be so good as to die this time..." He aimed the ball. Simon braced himself to dodge.

Chapter Thirty-Four

The grinding of stone on stone distracted Jessica from Simon's defense. Demdike's missile flew wide as all three turned their attention to the door. In the opening stood Foras, his green leather clothes torn and burned, his skin blackened in places. Foras stepped into the room and stood still until the door had sealed behind him.

Jessica's hand covered her mouth. How had Demdike inflicted such damage on one as powerful as Foras?

"Quite the little party we are having." Demdike's cool voice wavered. "It seems I was less than thorough with you, William. Although if you wouldn't mind waiting your turn, I have to deal with this upstart first. I won't keep you waiting too long."

"There is no escape from this place." Foras strode forward to stand beside Jessica.

"Really?" Demdike's grin returned. "Whichever of you sealed the room, it matters not at all. When I kill the originator of the magic, the spell will cease. I will be free."

"It is not just we three you have to kill, then." Foras climbed into the stone bowl and looked down on Demdike. Eleven demons stepped from their hiding places. Fire raged in the circular trough.

Demdike snarled. "So you have called help. They will vanish when you die." He spread his fingers wide. A filament of green, shot through with black, formed at the tip of each.

"Not so. The circle was broken. None need return to Hell." Foras folded his arms.

"What? Then you are fools indeed, to let these creatures loose in the world." Demdike's filaments lengthened and whipped at the air.

Jessica grabbed Simon's arm as he stumbled against her. His sweat mingled with the stench of charred flesh. His pain showed in his eyes when he turned them to her.

"Jessica. I am sorry." Tears formed in Simon's eyes.

Marchosias, Amon and Phenex walked through the flames and surrounded Demdike.

"Tell me it's not true, Simon. Tell me you didn't know about my father." Jessica clung to Simon's arm. Above her, Demdike's filaments reached for Foras. Foras made no move to prevent them.

Simon closed his eyes. "I could not bring myself to tell you."

Jessica pushed him away. Bile rose in her throat. Simon was the one man she had trusted. Not only was he a pawn of Demdike, he had concealed her father's death. She should have grieved for him. Now she had nothing.

"You cannot succeed." Foras spoke in a confident tone. He smiled at Demdike as the eight demons remaining outside the flames began to chant.

Marchosias and Amon breathed flame at Demdike's feet. Phenex rose into the air and spread golden wings as he transformed into a fiery bird. Jessica shielded her eyes from the heat and light flowing from him.

"I always succeed. If not in this body, then in another." Demdike's voice deepened. The hem of his robe ignited.

"Why don't they stop him?" Simon held the edge of the stone bowl. He lifted his hands away as a jet-black bar appeared, connecting the bowl with its upturned counterpart above. More bars flew between the top and bottom of the construction.

Jessica took a step back, and then stepped forward again. Trapped between the surrounding flame and the bowl, she could only watch as the black bars surrounded Foras.

Simon grabbed at her arm. "That thing is in Demdike, isn't it? The black thing I saw. The Golab."

"Yes." Jessica brushed him aside. She stared at Foras, at his ripped clothing, his burned skin, and wondered at the smile on his face. Did he feel no pain?

"Why don't they stop it?" Simon gestured at Marchosias, Amon and Phenex. They deluged Demdike in flame, but Demdike simply laughed. The green filaments from his fingers turned to pure black. They attached themselves to Foras, to his arms, his legs, his torso.

A darkness formed in the air over Demdike's head. He raised his hands and transferred the filaments to the shapeless mass. Outside the flames, the chant increased in speed. The black bars surrounding Foras thickened.

Jessica narrowed her eyes. The mass flowing from Demdike's head, framed against the fire that raged around them, pulsated and wavered. It now held the filaments that connected it to Foras.

"Make them stop it." Simon screamed the words. "The thing will get into Foras. With his power, we will all be doomed."

The pulsating shape paused. Demdike spoke through the fire that consumed his body.

"Foras? Then I have been deceived."

Foras turned his head to glare at Simon. His eyes burned with leaf-green fury. "Idiot. It cannot take me. I am simply bait."

Jessica closed her eyes. She understood why Foras had allowed the Golab to inflict so much damage. It had to believe he was human, so it would try to take his body. That was the only way to get it into the trap. Simon had ruined everything.

Simon shrieked. Jessica opened her eyes.

The Golab struck Simon with several of its filaments. Even as they detached from Foras, the filaments crossed between the bars of the bowl and attached themselves to Simon. Foras leaped from the bowl.

Demdike's body crumbled into ash. Freed of its former host, the Golab launched itself across the bowl. The demon's chant increased in both pitch and volume. More bars appeared, thickening and blending together as they grew.

"With luck, we will still have it." Foras whispered into Jessica's ear. She pressed her body against his, thankful for his solid presence.

The Golab passed between the bars of the trap and enveloped Simon's body.

Chapter Thirty-Five

The touch of the Golab cut like a sword of ice into Simon's skin. Where he had no skin, the pain lanced into sinew and bone. Simon fell to his knees. More of the Golab's tendrils struck him. With every new touch, Simon's mind crumbled. The black bars that separated him from the main mass of the Golab increased in number and thickness, but the creature flowed between them as easily as water through a grate. Simon wished for a quick death on Alloces' sword, but that option had, he knew, expired.

The darkness descended and bled into him. It cackled along his nerves and laughed in his guts. Simon's mind was pulled and pushed; pieces came off and drifted into the parasite's hungry maw.

"Now, Simon. You know what you must do." Elizabeth's voice echoed in his head. "I will give you the strength to do it."

The creature roared within him. It tore at his thoughts, pummeled his reason. Simon stared into the thickening bars of the trap.

Trap. That was what the bowl must be. Foras said he was bait. The Golab had to be within the trap.

Simon's abyss opened before him. That comforting oblivion called. It promised to hide him from the monster that ravaged his body from within. Simon shook his head. *Not yet.*

He had to hurry. He knew, without knowing why, that he had to get into the stone bowl before the bars became one. Before the trap closed. Simon forced his legs to stand.

The Golab snarled in his mind. It pulled at his muscles. It pushed his bones. It would accept no less than submission, absolute and unconditional. Simon took a step forward.

"Simon..." Jessica's eyes were wide. She leaned back into the protective embrace of the demon Foras.

Simon tried to smile, but could not tell if he succeeded. Foras nodded at him, grim-faced. Simon grasped the bowl of the trap with both hands. The three demons who had incinerated Demdike watched, unmoving. Outside the flames, the chant continued.

Simon pulled himself over the lip of the bowl. He lifted his legs so that he was completely encased in the black bars of Jessica's trap. The Golab within him screamed its fury. Simon laughed at its impotent rage.

I have done so many things wrong. Let this be an end to them all.

Simon closed his eyes and surrendered himself to the abyss.

Chapter Thirty-Six

Jessica watched the black shape disappear into Simon's body. With her eyes half-closed, she could make out his aura, even against the flames. Blue, tinged with the red of pain, it shrank as the Golab absorbed his life. Simon fell to his knees and clenched his teeth. Jessica's eyes widened as Simon's aura reappeared. This time there was no red. Pure sky blue surrounded him.

She pressed harder against Foras. His arms encircled her.

"He knows." Foras whispered the words in her ear.

Simon stood. His limbs jerked like a puppet's, in the hands of an inexpert master. He grasped the edges of the stone bowl and turned his face to hers.

"Simon..." She wanted to say, 'Don't'. She wanted to say, 'Stop', but there were no words left to say. Simon was lost to her, and she had refused him comfort in his last moments. No matter that he had betrayed her to Demdike, nor that he had concealed her father's death. He was Simon, and he had cared for her.

Jessica tried to lunge forward, to prevent Simon's action, but Foras held her. She sagged in his arms. Even if she managed to stop what Simon clearly intended, he was in the grip of the Golab. How he fought against it, she had no idea, but he surely could not maintain the battle for long.

Simon smiled. He heaved himself into the bowl and was immediately lost to sight within the column of darkness forming there. His legs protruded for a moment before he hauled them inside.

The final spaces closed. Between the twin bowls stood an ebony column which occupied their full width. The demons' chant ended. Phenex became a child once more. The trough of fire extinguished and eight demons approached the group within.

"It is done. Not as we had intended, but the Golab is trapped." Foras released his hold on Jessica. She felt no urge to pull away.

Jessica blinked away tears. "Simon. Can't you get him out of there?"

"It's too late." Orobas stood before her. "The trap is closed. Even if we could get him out, the Golab has destroyed his mind."

"What about Foras? How were you going to get him out?"

Jessica looked into Foras's eyes.

Orobas shuffled his feet.

"They were not." Foras set his jaw. "I was to remain in the trap with the creature."

"For three hundred years?" Jessica placed her hands on Foras's chest.

"It's not that long, really, for one of our kind." Bifrons' voice came from behind her.

"There are things we do not know about the creature." Foras rubbed his forehead. "We do not know how long it retains the memory of those it absorbs. When it is released, when the hybrid is ready to kill it, it might still have Demdike's powers. It might not."

"You would have spent three hundred years in there, to find that out?" Jessica shook her head. She could not imagine such sacrifice.

"There is more." Phenex looked up at her. For once, his eyes held a serious expression. "There is the matter of Baal."

Foras waved the little demon to silence. Jessica pressed her hands on his chest.

"Tell me, Foras."

Foras sniffed and looked away. "Baal will play a joke. I believe I know what it might be. If I had been within the trap, Baal would have had to wait for his amusements. By the time I emerged, you would be safe from the effects of his joke."

"Perhaps it is as well you escaped the snare." Marchosias said. "It would have angered Baal. He might have taken retribution on Jessica."

Foras sighed. "It does not matter now. I must submit to his amusements, whatever they may be." He closed his eyes. The skin on his face and hands healed, and the tears and rents in his clothing closed.

Jessica stood back, open-mouthed, and marveled at Foras's face, now as perfect as when she had first called him.

"Foras, you were burned." Jessica gasped the words.

"Illusion, for the most part." Foras checked his jacket. "The Golab would have known I was not human if his attacks had left no mark." He looked around at the other demons. "Our work here cannot be completed today. We must return to finish the Golab in three centuries. Maybe longer. Hold faith, and do not slip back into the darkness. If our numbers decline further, we may yet fail." He smiled. "My friends, go in peace. We have taken a step toward redemption this night. Now we have to wait until it is time for the second step."

"Where do we go?" Phenex stood beside Foras.

"The circle that called us was broken. We are free in this world."

Foras and Phenex moved away, continuing their conversation in low voices. Alloces faced Jessica, beside the old man she had seen in her lounge. The old man spoke.

"It is time to leave, and we have not even been introduced. I am Agares. It will be my task to find a suitable human host to occupy. I regret that you will not see the death of the Golab, but I am nonetheless pleased that you have survived this venture."

"Simon did not survive." Jessica choked on the words.

Alloces nodded. "There were too many deaths, but Simon Bulcock's actions have prevented the Golab from killing thousands."

Jessica's tears flowed unchecked. Orobas moved forward but Phenex stopped him. The demons withdrew from her and remained silent.

She wept for her mother. Finally, she could lay her mother's spirit to rest. Jessica had avenged her betrayal by Demdike and her death at the hands of the Golab. Jessica wept for her father, for his abrupt departure from her life and the new knowledge that he could never again be part of it.

She wept for Simon, for the pain he must have felt, knowing her father dead and lacking the courage to tell her. For his final sacrifice, for his strength and support over the years, Jessica wept.

When her sobs subsided, Foras laid his hand on her shoulder. "You must leave this place. The Golab will not escape unaided, but it will soon try to entice women to itself. It has that power, granted by Asmodeus. Once it has acclimatized to the trap, it will begin its lures."

Jessica allowed Foras to lead her to the door, which Phenex opened for them. At the threshold, she stopped and faced the demons.

"Thank you." She forced a smile. "What will you all do now?"

Andromalius, Phenex, Agares and Seere bowed to her.

"We can mingle with the people of your world and remain unnoticed, with a little care," Phenex said. "There is much to see."

Crocell joined them. "I have often wished to explore the waters of this world. Because of you, I am free to do so."

Orobas blinked his large eyes. "I will go with Phenex and the others, I think. They will not all fit on Seere's horse."

Malphas scratched his head with his trowel. "There is more work to do here. The house is not exactly as I would like. The haste of its construction has led to imperfections."

Amon, Marchosias and Alloces stepped forward. Amon spoke. "We three will travel together to the places where man does not venture. There is peace in such remote areas, and we are unlikely to be accepted by your people."

Jessica searched the group with her eyes. "What of Bifrons?"

Seere laughed. "Doubtless he will spin his web in a brothel somewhere." He glanced around. "Where is he? Already seeking suitable accommodation?"

"Here." Bifrons scuttled from the smoldering remains of Demdike to stop at Foras's feet. "I found this." He held up a black crystal, as big as Foras's fist. Its facets seemed to absorb rather than reflect the light that fell on them.

Foras took the crystal from Bifrons. He held it up and examined it. Jessica shied away from its foul aura.

"Demdike." Foras growled the word. "Or rather, his essence." He handed the crystal to Malphas. "Seal this, but make it outside the circle. Far from the house."

"Demdike is dead, Foras." Jessica watched the crystal as Malphas carried it past her, into the tunnel. "Isn't he?"

"The Golab has absorbed Demdike's soul." Foras drew a long breath. "However, when the Golab dies, all of the souls it now holds will be freed."

"So Demdike can return." Jessica ran her tongue over her suddenly-dry lips.

"His soul will be released, yes. That does not mean he can return. He will have to find his essence, and he will need a human body to possess. Malphas will hide the remains where they cannot be found." He placed his arm around Jessica's shoulders and squeezed. "You will never see him again."

Tears threatened to well in Jessica's eyes once more. She fought the tremble in her lip. One by one, the demons faded from view, each with a smile, some with a nod and a wave.

Amon slithered forward. "I have one last service to perform. I will let Foras know the extent of my work tomorrow." Amon winked one huge, circular eye and vanished.

Only Foras, Bifrons and Phenex remained. Jessica swallowed hard and knelt before Phenex and Bifrons. She took Phenex's hand.

"Thank you. Phenex. You were a great help to me at the start of this. I might have lost my mind without you." She took one of Bifron's little hands in her other hand, surprised to find she felt no revulsion at his touch. "And you, Bifrons. I nearly did lose my mind when we met, but I count you as a friend now."

Blushing, Bifrons lifted her hand to his mouth and kissed it. Phenex did the same. They both released her and stood back.

"Go now. I will seal this door before Bifrons and I take our leave." Phenex waved her away.

Foras took her arm and led her into the candlelit tunnel. They stood together as the door swung over the opening, turning away as it closed. As they walked along the tunnel, Foras blew out the candles they passed.

"What were you and Phenex talking about back there?" Jessica asked.

"He wanted to stay, to share Baal's payment. I forbade it."

"Why?"

"Because if Baal saw I had help, he would count his game spoiled. Your soul would be forfeit." He paused to blow out another candle. "I, or perhaps we, must face his amusement alone."

Jessica fell silent, and spoke no more throughout the long walk back to the house.

Chapter Thirty-Seven

In the basement, Foras closed the tunnel entrance and muttered a few words until it blended with the brickwork of the wall. When he finished, no indication remained to suggest the existence of a door. He nodded and climbed the stairs. Jessica followed.

Something ran past her legs, something small and black. Jessica shrieked and nearly lost her footing. The thing stopped at the top of the stairs and mewed at her.

"Belson. You scared me half to death." Jessica put her hand over her heaving chest. She caught the amusement in Foras's eyes before he turned away and continued to the hallway.

Jessica allowed herself a chuckle as she followed. A room filled with demons held no terrors for her, but a fast-moving cat had nearly stopped her heart. She stepped into the hallway and collided with Foras, who had stopped, staring at something near the front door. Belson had disappeared.

It looked like a deer with its tail on fire. Curiously, the blaze at its rear seemed not to disturb it at all. Jessica moved toward the deer but Foras held her back.

"It is Furfur, loyal to Baal," he said. "I see Baal has wasted no time. He must be anxious to enjoy his joke."

The deer walked forward, its huge brown eyes fixed on Foras. It flicked its tail, spiraling smoke toward the ceiling. Foras's eyes widened. His jaw dropped open. Jessica turned her attention to Furfur just as it moved its eyes to meet her gaze.

Inner peace filled her. She felt only love, and her developing attraction to Foras became infatuation. Within those brown deer eyes, Jessica forgot what Foras was. He became a man, the man she had always hoped to find.

Furfur lowered its head and retreated. Flame spread from its tail, engulfing its entire body, and then it vanished with a flash of light that made Jessica shield her eyes.

"Was that it?" Jessica looked up at Foras. She admired the muscles bunched beneath the leather sleeves of his jerkin, and gasped at his long black hair. "Was that Baal's joke?"

"I cannot resist. I gave my word." Foras turned his luminous eyes to hers. Desire burned within them. He took her in his arms and kissed her.

The heat of him flowed into her body as he held her close. Jessica sighed as Foras lifted her from the ground and carried her upstairs.

Chapter Thirty-Eight

Rain lashed the windows. Jessica opened her eyes and pulled the blankets closer around her. The air was warm, but the sound of the rain made her want to stay in bed. She reached out for Foras, but his side of the bed was cold. He must have risen some time ago.

Closing her eyes, Jessica smiled as she remembered the night before. Over the last few days she had feared for her life almost continuously, but it was over now. To have survived the experience should have been reward enough, but for Jessica there was more.

She had found love, in the most unlikely of places. She loved Foras, and he loved her. To think she had been terrified when she first summoned him here. He was so gentle, so caring, and so wonderful. Jessica yawned through her smile and stretched.

Now Foras was gone. Gripped with sudden concern, Jessica clambered from the bed, scooped her dress from the floor and pulled it over her head. All the other demons had vanished, their task completed.

Perhaps Foras was now in whatever realm these sprits occupied, bragging of his conquest. Her face heated. Tears formed in her eyes as she imagined demonic laughter at her expense. Bestiality was the word Baal had used. The recollection stung as she hauled open the bedroom door.

At the rail overlooking the hallway, Jessica paused. Foras sat on the bottom steps of the stairs, talking with Amon and Malphas. Her heart pounded. He was still here. Wiping the tears from her eyes, Jessica descended the stairs.

Amon noticed her descent and twisted his toothed owl-face into something that could have been a smile. Foras turned his head. Seeing her, he stood, his face serious.

"Foras? Is something wrong?" Jessica reached his side and linked her arm in his. He made no move, either to return the gesture or to push her away.

"Amon has news. Good news," Foras said.

"Indeed I have." Amon's tail whipped. "I have touched the

thoughts of this Lord West. His mind was still malleable from Demdike's fading influence, so I made some, ah, improvements to his memory."

"Really?" Jessica struggled to maintain interest in Amon's words while she wondered at Foras's indifference.

"He now believes you to be the instrument of Demdike's destruction, and his freedom. You will be rewarded in a few days, with a gift."

Jessica nodded, uncaring. Foras was all the gift she needed.

"This land will be yours. For you and your family, forever. So you can pass the legacy of care down the generations until we return."

"Excellent. I will build a wall to surround the land. That will reduce the burden on the Hiding, and protect the circle if it should ever fail." Malphas hopped away, his trowel held high.

"I have no family." Jessica pursed her lips. Beside her, Foras stiffened at her words.

"You will." Amon winked one of his circular black eyes and backed away. "That is my news. Now, I will take my leave. Goodbye once more, Jessica. Foras, I will see you again." He moved away and faded, becoming transparent before disappearing like smoke in the wind.

Jessica turned to Foras. "What did he mean?"

Foras bowed his head, the green in his eyes bright. "You will have a family, Jessica. You are pregnant."

"What?" Releasing Foras, Jessica placed both hands on her stomach. "How?"

Foras tilted his head to one side and raised one eyebrow.

"Well, yes." Flustered, Jessica turned away. "But how can you know, so soon?"

"I see the life growing in you. Part you, and part me. You know what that means?"

Jessica looked at the floor. Its intricate mosaic seemed distant, inconsequential. "It means you will stay?"

"It means I have to stay. That is Baal's joke."

"Joke?" Jessica whirled, fury rising in her. "You think this is a joke? Toying with my feelings, leaving me pregnant and alone?"

"I am not leaving." Foras's eyes burned, drawing her into their green aura. "I am not laughing. This prank of Baal's has consequences beyond the immediately obvious."

Jessica narrowed her eyes. "What consequences?"

"The feelings Furfur placed in you are also in me. I did not make love to you for Baal's amusement. I did it because I wanted to. I still want to."

Fury melted from Jessica's thoughts as she moved toward him.

"Don't you understand?" Foras turned his back to her. "Are you blind to the cruelty of Baal's entertainment?"

"What do you mean, Foras? We are together. We can be happy."

"For a time. You are mortal. I am not. Baal sent Furfur to rekindle feelings I have long suppressed. Once before, I watched a woman age and die, while I remained unchanged." Foras lowered his head.

"There is the child." Jessica bit her lip. She had been blind to her own selfishness. Foras would have to watch as she withered away, trapped here for the amusement of a king of Hell. He had given himself to this fate, to save her life. Her cheeks burned at the memory of her earlier suspicions.

Foras faced her. "We will produce a hybrid child, Jessica. A Nephilim. The child will live for several hundred years. He will be strong—"

"He? You know it is to be a boy?"

Foras smiled down at her. "They always are." He sighed. "I am bound to this earth now, to this place, as long as our son lives. The Nephilim cannot be left to his own devices, untrained. Some of us made that mistake once, long ago. I cannot be responsible for a repeat of that action."

Jessica reveled in the warmth of Foras as she rested her head on his chest. He suffered, she knew, and he would suffer further. Baal had arranged for Foras to repeat the error that had resulted in his expulsion from Heaven. Even when she died, Foras would have to remain with their child, a constant reminder of herself.

Just as the Golab was trapped below the garden, Foras was trapped above it. A lone tear trickled over Jessica's cheek.

Foras lifted the tear with his finger and inspected it.

"I will never understand how you make water flow from your eyes." Foras rubbed his finger and thumb together. "I think I am beginning to understand why."

About the Author:

H. K. Hillman is a self-employed researcher, also known as a rogue scientist, who works with dangerous and stinky things and would rather write for a living. He has produced a number of short stories but has now let his natural verbosity blossom with the writing of novels.

On the internet he exists in many forms, none of them really him. One such is Phineas Dume, who can be found at http://docdume.blogspot.com/ and contacted at docdume@gmail.com.

Also from Eternal Press:

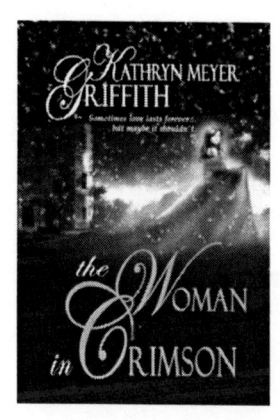

The Woman in Crimson
by Kathryn Meyer Griffith

eBook ISBN: 9781615721979
Print ISBN: 9781615721986

Romance, Horror, Vampire
Novel of 96,494 words

Sometimes love lasts forever...but maybe it shouldn't. Willowwind, a beautiful Civil War era bed and breakfast, is run by a loving couple, Adrian and Caroline Stone, but it's also haunted by a long-dead Civil War era vampiress, Lilith, who believes the man, Adrian, is her reincarnated soldier/lover and will do anything to have him, body-heart-and soul, for her own again, no matter how many she must kill. But Adrian's wife, Caroline, along with the help of the ghost of her dead father, will do anything to make sure that doesn't happen.

Also from Eternal Press:

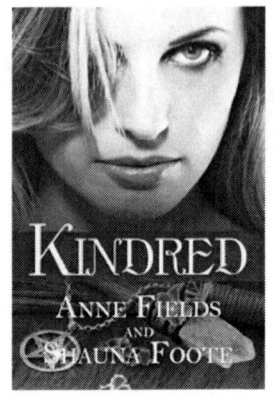

Kindred
by Anne Fields & Shauna Foote

eBook ISBN: 9781615722211
Print ISBN: 9781615722228

Paranormal, Dark Fantasy, Witch
Short Novel of 55,146 words

Three close friends are reunited through fate and magick. Tormented by their haunted dreams and visions of another lifetime past, they are led on a quest to find their true selves and to change their destinies. But, little did they know that attempting to alter fate and time offers consequences they never could have imagined.

CPSIA information can be obtained at www.ICGtesting.com
260996BV00001B/3/P